Bristol Short Prize Anthology

Volume Eleven

BS11
BRISTOL SHORT STORY PRIZE

tangent books

Bristol Short Story Prize Anthology Volume 11

First published 2018 by Tangent Books

Tangent Books
Unit 5.16 Paintworks
Bristol
BS4 3EH
0117 972 0645
www.tangentbooks.co.uk

Email: richard@tangentbooks.co.uk

ISBN: 9781910089781

Cover designed by Valentina Vinci

Layout designed by Dave Oakley, Arnos Design
www.arnosdesign.co.uk

Printed and bound by ScandinavianBook.co.uk
c/o LaserTryk.co.uk Ltd.
Hamilton House, Mabledon Place
Bloomsbury, WC1H 9BB

A CIP catalogue record for this book is available from the British Library

www.tangentbooks.co.uk

www.bristolprize.co.uk

Contents

Introduction

Writing is an act usually done quietly, privately, internally: typing at your desk, scribbling in the corner of a café, or letting your imagination secretly run wild while stuck at your day job. It takes a lot of solitary striving before it garners gratitude, or applause, or even a paycheck. A writer works inside a room, inside a Word document, inside her head. It then takes great courage to finally say – to yourself, to a friend, to a judging panel – "I'm a writer."

So, congratulations to the 20 writers within the pages of this anthology, to the 40 writers on the longlist, to the more than 2,000 writers who were brave enough to send a story off to the Bristol Short Story Prize this year. You are all writers, aloud, in broad daylight.

A careful team of readers considered every entry and chose among them a longlist of 40 standouts, which was then passed along to our judging panel. I joined editor Lucy Cowie and writers Roshi Fernando and Polly Ho-Yen in reading and selecting half of those, and then agonizing over the top three, which this year became four.

Our stories sharing third place are stylistically very different from each other, but we felt unanimously that they both needed to be commended. Of Helen Rye's *Transposition*, Roshi Fernando says, 'this story addresses beautifully the emotional rush away from trauma into the daily life of a foreign world which is unwelcoming, in a succinct, thought-provoking and gut-wrenching manner.' Lucy Cowie describes *Little Yellow Planes* by Zeus Sumra as 'skillfully using a child's perspective to cast light on economic injustice and explore the value of storytelling.'

Polly Ho-Yen calls Chloe Wilson's second-place-winning story, *Powerful Owl*, 'such an insightful and accomplished story that I reread it over and over, relishing in its tight characterisation and claustrophobic setting.'

And our first-place winner, Dizz Tate's perspicuous, bittersweet *Cowboy Boot*, gives us a novel's worth of narrative in less than 1,500 words, showing what ripples after one man dies.

The experiences, settings, voices, and locations of the writers varied widely, with entries from across the world. Within these pages, the reader gets to travel to the past and the future, to destinations close and far, and, for a few thousand words at a time, to dwell inside the minds of dislocated children, grieving mothers, despairing lovers, a father with Alzheimer's, a pregnant woman with a decision to make, a stutterer, a vampire, the occupants of a single avenue, as well as refugees, journalists, and travellers making sense of the shrinking globe. Some stories let us escape into worlds unknown; some dive unflinchingly into the tenuous-seeming state of the world we know.

This 11th edition of the Bristol Short Story Prize anthology binds this broad spectrum with a whimsical portrait of Bristol by Valentina Vinci, selected as part of a cover design project with Illustration students at the University of the West of England. Thanks to all those who entered – we received so many stunning designs – and thank you to UWE course leaders Chris Hill and Jonathan Ward for their commitment to the project.

And now, here they are: 20 stories that now jump from private endeavour to public audience. I'm delighted to welcome them into the world, and hope you enjoy each one as much as we did.

Kate Johnson

1ˢᵗ Prize
Dizz Tate

Dizz Tate is a writer currently living in London, after growing up in Orlando, Florida. She has been previously published in the *Wrong Quarterly, Squawk Back, Arachne Press,* and *Femmeuary.* In 2017, she was featured in *3:AM Magazine, No Tokens Journal,* and *Corda.* She has work forthcoming in *Prism International,* and *Dazed.* She is currently working on her first novel.

Cowboy Boot

The jungle gym was a gift from Richard Turnball to his little stepdaughter, two weeks before his plane went down on a private flight from Cleveland to Colorado. Turnball was a flight attendant, which Mary, who lived opposite, had always politely thought was a profession for ladies, no offence intended.

The bodies could not be identified, mangled with metal and burns, but they retrieved a few molars, and found a white, gold-trimmed cowboy boot a few miles away on a mountain, miraculously whole, and undeniably Turnball's, his name having even been printed on the bottom by his doting wife, Jillian, some months before. The cowboy boot was delivered to Jillian by First-Class mail, and became somewhat of a sensation in the state press, the Miracle Boot From the Mountain. Jillian was not in any of the photographs, but her little girl was, holding the boot and looking morose. Mary thought this doubly distasteful, as after all, she was not even his true child. Jillian wailed noisily for weeks after she received the boot, even though his death had been pretty much certain for months already. Sometimes Mary thought she understood this behaviour, and sometimes she didn't understand it at all.

The jungle gym from Turnball was right next to Mary's house, in the only empty lot in the neighbourhood. The forces that ran the community had wanted to uproot it back across to the Turnball's driveway ('Why would he dump it on someone else's property?' they asked each other, over and over, 'He's got a perfectly good yard!') but after his death, the jungle gym remained, and the lot stayed empty, out of some form of respect, though none of the kids even used it, there being the community centre just three streets away with a playground three times the size.

It was some weeks after the boot delivery when Mary watched Jillian and her little girl cross the street toward her porch and the lot. She sat up a little straighter. Jillian held a shovel and her little girl held the famous boot. The girl darted up the jungle gym and sat on the top of the slide, holding the boot like a baby, while Jillian began to dig a hole at the bottom. Jillian was a small, birdy woman, and the digging took her a long time. She could barely shift the dirt, hard-packed as it was from the cold.

Mary sat in the chair in her porch and watched her as she dug more and more wildly, sweat forming a thick sheen on her forehead. She thought of the times she had seen Turnball careening down the street in the family Ford. She had seen him passed out in every front yard in the street – everyone knew he'd turned thick from liquor. A few times he had been with other people, shadows in the passenger seat. They would park in front of the jungle gym and seem to just talk. Mary was not fooled. She had seen enough to know that talking could be the most dangerous kind of work.

She had been working out how to tell Jillian about her husband's indiscretions when he died in the plane crash. She felt both relieved and a little bitter at her missed opportunity. Mary was known for passing on damaging information at the most brittle of times. She saw a lot – sitting all day in her screened-in porch, the Turnball's opposite, Georgia May and her little pretty family next to them. The other house she could see most clearly was the rental house – full of strangers for weeks in the summer, and thus a cauldron of gossip. Mary found the vacationers fascinating.

They were so odd. One young couple liked to climb on the roof and sunbathe naked. Another family wore turbans. Another had a little boy and girl who played at murdering each other in the driveway, acting out a hundred different deaths, while their father stood in the doorway, filming them on his phone.

While Jillian dug the hole, the little girl sucked her thumb on the top of the slide. She'd suck for a second, then spit over her shoulder. Suck and spit. Disgusting, thought Mary, but the mother just kept pushing her shovel into the dirt and did not chastise the girl.

Some of the other mothers came and stood around. Mrs. Hutchinson, who was Mary's age, and she thought, too old to be involved in these types of tragedies, brought a bottle of whisky, which she passed around in paper cups. The mothers stood around Jillian who continued to dig as though they were not there. No one offered to help her, but occasionally one or the other would dart a quick hand to slap Jillian's shoulder. Mary thought they looked like crows, ravenous to peck at a non-existent seed.

Mrs. Hutchinson came up to Mary's screen door after a while and tipped the whisky bottle to her. 'Can't tempt you, Mary?' she said. Mary shook her head, pulled her blanket to her neck, but Mrs. Hutchinson opened the screen door anyway, sat cross-legged like a child on the floor of her porch.

'You're a saint, lady Mary,' she said, slurring. Mary looked past her, watched as Georgia May, the prettiest woman on the street, with a teenagers face at forty, swung an arm round Jillian.

'Looks deep enough,' said Georgia May.

Jillian's face scrunched itself up. She sat on the ground, looked at the little girl who took her thumb from her mouth, slid down the slide, expertly braking with her feet to stop herself at the bottom before hitting the hole. She placed the boot in the earth, stuck her thumb back in her mouth, spat.

'Aren't you a little old for thumb-sucking?' Called Mrs. Hutchinson to the girl. Mary blushed. The girl looked at them for a second, then down again at the hole. She put her hands in her coat pockets.

'Oh, shut up, would you?' said Mary to Mrs. Hutchinson. The jungle gym shined in the winter sunlight. She strained to hear Jillian.

'Perhaps we should have burnt it,' she said. 'But burying seemed more – oh, I don't know –'

'Significant,' said Georgia May. She took the shovel gently from Jillian's hands, gave her a plastic cup to hold.

Georgia May's daughter, a cheeky kid in a boy's tuxedo jacket, hair curling in under her chin, wandered up to the hole. Mary watched as she whispered something to Jillian's little girl, who looked up at her, expressionless, then offered a dazzling smile.

Oh, I wish I knew what she said, thought Mary.

'The little ones are so much different than us, aren't they, Mary?' said Mrs. Hutchinson. 'They're surely not gonna listen to you when you tell them about their cheating husbands. They'll probably be the cheaters themselves.'

'Oh, be quiet, you drunk old bat,' said Mary, and Mrs. Hutchinson laughed.

'Look up!' cried Georgia May's little girl, suddenly. Georgia May, Jillian, Mrs. Hutchinson, Mary, and the few other women all looked up. A sheer arc of starlings contracted and expanded across the waxy blue sky.

'There's Richard,' said Jillian. 'There's Richard waving to me.'

Mrs. Hutchinson tutted, and said, low under her breath so only Mary could hear, 'That old fag is a boot in the ground and nothing else now.'

Mary chuckled. Pushing herself from her chair, she walked to the other side of the screen porch and sat in the chair that used to belong to her husband. She still got a faint sense of unease sitting in it – once, years before he died, she had sunk herself down into it and refused to move, even while he worked himself up into a fit, ('That's my chair! My chair!'), his hands in fists he was never going to throw.

'Sit in a chair, for goodness sake, woman,' she said now to Mrs. Hutchinson, who struggled upright and sat in the vacated chair, her feet curled girlishly beneath her.

Mary looked over the length of the street, the icy black tarmac and the beige houses lined up, neat and well-behaved looking as show dogs. She looked for the girls, but they had gone, disappeared into one house or another, and she thought for a long time while Mrs. Hutchinson slurred her way to sleep beside her, just what it was that the one had whispered to the other, to make her smile that way.

2nd Prize
Chloe Wilson

Chloe Wilson is the author of two poetry collections, *The Mermaid Problem* and *Not Fox Nor Axe*, which was shortlisted for the Kenneth Slessor Prize for Poetry and the Judith Wright Calanthe Award. She received equal first prize in the 2016 Josephine Ulrick Poetry Prize, and was shortlisted for the 2017 Commonwealth Short Story Prize.

Powerful Owl

The first part of Maya to wash up on shore was a foot. The cop they sent to break the news arrived on our doorstep with her cap under her arm. She knocked on the flyscreen. The mesh shimmied under her knuckles.

When we opened the door, flies came in.

Her shoes stuck to the linoleum in the kitchen. She accepted a glass of soft drink, and soon its neon green transferred to her tongue.

'You sure it's her?' said my mother.

'We're sure,' the cop said.

'What about Cameron? Where was he?' I asked.

Mum shot me a look.

The cop said they were not treating the circumstances as suspicious. Maya had been seen alone on the beach that night.

My mother didn't ask how Maya's body had come apart the way it did. So I asked instead.

'It's just the tide,' the cop said. 'It's natural.'

In the end Mum had to identify the foot, as she was Maya's sister and the closest living relative she had left.

Other parts washed up over the weeks that followed: an arm, a thigh, part of a torso with the spine hanging out like a braid. Eventually the same cop came back and said, 'I think this is the best we're going to do.'

Maya went into the furnace in a cardboard coffin.

My mother, once Maya was half a plastic container of ash, shook her straight back into the ocean she'd returned from.

'Serves her right,' she said.

Soon after that I decided to leave. Home was starting to jangle my nerves. Watching the road become molten in the afternoon mirage. Wiping grit from my neck, licking salt from my upper lip. It had been years since I had noticed the dull pounding of the waves, but after Maya died it got to a point where I would lie awake unable to block out their constant, regular arrival, the wash and drag of it.

And we had other unending rhythms in that town: my mother lighting a fresh cigarette with a dying one, the race-caller's mounting panic coming over the car radio, the burr of static underneath. There were Saturday nights at the pub drinking vodka and raspberry until it came up in a pink rush against a wall, and boys who would holler their encouragement and kiss me anyway as though this was a tender favour.

One Sunday, I put an ad on a website. I left it there a week. There was only one reply.

So this was who went to live in the hills, I thought.

How old was he? Forty-ish, I guessed, though he was thin enough and handsome enough to make his age seem like an advantage. His shirt was unironed. His lips might have been too broad, forming a rubbery oval like a clown's mouth, but he hid them with a beard. His bald spot wasn't alarming; it wouldn't have been larger than a one dollar coin.

He gestured towards the child, who was sitting on a Turkish rug in a room lined with book cases. White sunlight filtered in through the glass doors which led to the garden.

'She's a good kid,' he said. 'I can't imagine she'll give you much trouble.'
I was relieved to hear him use a pronoun. The baby was dressed in sombre grey and white, and her short black hair provided me with no clues whatsoever. Her name, Lee, hadn't helped.

She wasn't so much playing as she was grabbing at the elegant things which surrounded her.

'She keeps putting things in her mouth,' he said. 'You'll have to watch that.'

I assured him that I would.

My references were as excellent as they were fabricated. My friends, all childless, had assured him that I was conscientious, responsible, caring, patient. I was none of these things. But I was cheap.

His name was Marc, and he reminded me that it was spelled with a 'c'.

'Ok,' I said.

'I know you must have seen that in my emails. It feels silly to point it out. But it makes a difference.'

When I didn't reply, he continued. 'A "k" sounds harder. Like *ark*.' He pushed out the 'k' percussively. 'People always mispronounce it.'

'That must be annoying,' I said.

He showed me around the house. He walked me through an open plan dining room and kitchen, the living room where the baby played. There was no television. The couches faced one another.

Upstairs, there was the child's room, and then there were the doors he didn't open: his bedroom, his office.

'No shoes in the house by the way,' he said. 'Sorry. I should have mentioned it earlier.'

He looked at me while I leaned down and unlaced my sneakers. I'd thought them clean enough, but now could see the way grime had worked its way into the stitching.

When I was in my socks, he continued down the hallway to a closed white door.

'This is your room,' he said, opening it.

It was a like a room in a nun's cloister. Clean and white, with an oak child's wardrobe and a white single bed. A chest of three drawers sat beneath the window; on it was a tiny vase holding a single twig of eucalyptus. Marc explained that the bathroom next door could be for my exclusive use. He would confine himself to his en-suite.

'That's kind of you,' I said.

I stepped to the window and scanned the view: the rambling garden, the shambles of uneven grass.

'It's very nice,' I said. 'Your house.'

He walked into the room, pressed down lightly on the bed with a splayed hand.

'We like it.'

I could see the dimples of his fingers in the quilt cover.

It occurred to me later that 'arc' could also be spelled with a 'c'. Science was one of the subjects I hadn't failed. I remembered learning that an arc is the visible jolt of electricity between one point and another, that jagging blue-white path energy takes when it's trying to find the fastest way from one point to the next.

As for the wife, I never saw her. That's not completely true: I saw her all the time, smiling obligingly out of framed photographs. She was away on some kind of sabbatical – archaeological, I think, although that might just be because they had a lot of artefacts around which looked like they'd been dug out of somewhere: limestone and soapstone, clay and sand.

He, Marc, worked from home during the day except for Fridays, when he went to a University in the city to teach a seminar on torts. When he said this word I pictured cakes. I had worked in a bakery for a while. To me, tortes were dense eastern European things that sat like stones in their boxes when I packed them up.

He smiled when he corrected me.

'No,' he said. 'A tort is a wrongdoing.'

Still I pictured layers of dense wintery sweetness as foreign as snow.

Marc explained further.

'Say a man is driving a car, and the car veers off the road and over a cliff,' he said. The baby was in bed and we were drinking dandelion tea, a strong, swampy brew that stank like the chicory my great-grandmother drank. He was on one couch. I was on the other.

'Say the man dies. Who's to blame? The driver? The car? The roads authority?'

'No-one,' I said. 'It's an accident.'

That made him laugh, a soft near-soundless chuckle.

'You probably wouldn't like my class,' he said.

'What's the answer?'

'Well, that depends. The average students would say the driver. The better students would think of a way to sue the manufacturer of the car, or whoever maintained the roads. The best students say things like – "well, for all we know a bee flew into the car." They don't accept things at face value.'

I didn't know what to say. I was thinking of that car smashing through the barrier and launching over the edge. I was thinking of the pinch of a bee's sting when it lodges in your calf; the way rubber screeches when it's burned into a wild curve on the asphalt.

When Marc was working at home, my job was to maintain silence in the house. This meant keeping the baby quiet.

How long and slow the days became that spring. Often I spent entire afternoons speaking to no-one but the baby. At night I would lie still and hear the calls of nocturnal birds – trilling and knocking sounds, throaty sounds, calls that sounded like choking. And occasionally a 'Woo hoo... woo hoo....woo hoo,' called long and loud over the night.

Marc had been correct about one thing. The baby didn't give me any trouble. She was good, quiet, a warm little weight that I picked up as frequently out of my own boredom as because she cried or reached up.

But though Lee was a good baby, even good babies cry, and though I jiggled her and sang to her and cooed and patted her back, sometimes she would wail and wail for a reason I couldn't discern.

Early on, at one of these times, Marc descended the stairs until he was standing on the bottom step, his toes in cashmere socks curling over its edge.

'Perhaps a walk?' he said.

'To where?'

There wasn't much where he lived. No shops, at least not in walking distance. No beach, no library.

He waved a hand irritably towards the trees outside.

'She likes it out there,' he said.

I went outside with the pram and walked Lee to the end of the street. I could see the path that led to the trees, which shivered and made a hissing sound in the pollen littered breeze. But I had no interest in approaching them.

In the end I settled for walking up and down the street.

Eventually, the baby stopped crying.

I watched her plump face, creaseless in sleep. It struck me that it was impossible to remember being a person to whom nothing terrible had happened. A person to whom nothing had happened to at all.

I don't remember what I was thinking when I wheeled Lee's pram to the middle of the road. There was no traffic. It's not as though I thought anything was coming. I just wheeled it out and walked back to the footpath and watched for a minute, or maybe two.

Lee didn't stir or snap awake. She slept on, oblivious.

Maya and I were both flinchers.

Maya had liked Cameron's height. Six six, she had said to me on the beach one day, when we were sinking one beer after another and letting the empties roll down the dunes. He makes me feel like a baby doll.

The nun's room began to smell like me. The door was closed all day. Whenever I entered I could smell the scent of my own sealed and sleeping body. I was surprised every time by its mustiness, by its potency.

One day I went into the nearest town and bought a candle to dissipate this odour. I paid for it out of the cash Marc gave me. That was our arrangement, too, an arrangement I'd agreed on. Cash in an envelope with nothing printed on it, once a week, usually a Friday. When I can smell cash on someone's hands – that sweaty, grubby smell – I still think of him.

I'd bought the candle at one of the nicer shops. *Sea salt and cedar*. That was a Saturday, my day off. I had the night off too but there was nothing to do. I came home in the late afternoon to find Marc reading on the couch, one long thin leg slung over the other.

'Staying in tonight?'

'I thought I'd have a quiet one.'

I came back downstairs later in the evening. Lee had been put to bed. Marc was cooking, using a peeler to take skin-thin strips off a long white vegetable that I'd never seen before.

'It's a daikon,' he said when he saw me looking. 'Have you had dinner?'

Even now I couldn't tell you what he made. I know there was no meat in it. I know he was very keen on never harming the earth or the creatures that roamed it. And I knew this included the creatures that I considered brainless – the mussels we'd pried from under the pier when I was young, the oysters we stole from farms when the tide went out.

He suggested that we eat on the patio. I followed him outside.

He asked questions about me – siblings? University? And what do you want to do eventually? I heard how narrow my life sounded, as its components were paraded one by one in front of him. The unhemmed edges of my education. My one overseas trip to Bali. My family, working in dull jobs; a deckhand, a dental nurse, a receptionist.

Eventually I heard it again: that low 'woo hoo' coming at intervals, something between a voice and a woodwind instrument.

'What is that?' I said.

'An owl,' he said. 'The Powerful Owl, to be exact.'

We sat in silence for a moment, listening to it.

'Reminds me of one of the cases we discuss in class,' he said.

'Oh?'

'It's not a tort exactly, but the students like it. So – a man was accused of murdering his wife. She was found at the bottom of the staircase in a pool of blood. He had motives – they had been arguing, and he stood to inherit a substantial sum from life insurance.

'Anyway, there were wounds on her head. They thought the husband had struck her with a fire poker or some such. This was in the US, by the way – '

'So they electrocuted him?'

Good, I thought, imagining the electricity lighting him up from the inside, those blue-white jolts finding their way.

'Not quite. See, the wife had hanks of her own hair in each hand. And there were little feathers too. And the shape of the wounds wasn't really consistent with a poker. Expert ornithologists said they looked like a gash caused by an owl's talons. Also this was in the mating season when owls are at their most aggressive.'

'So... an owl did it?'

He shrugged, turning down his clown mouth in practiced uncertainty.

'What do you think? That's what I'd ask my students. Who's responsible? Who's at fault? How many ways can you interpret the facts?'

Later I searched for information about owls. I learned that they did indeed swoop on humans, mistaking us for rats or mice. I learned that prey never saw or heard them coming, because their feathers were designed for silence: serrated on one edge, fringed on the other.

I learned that a half-kilogram owl could land on a mouse with the equivalent force of a ten-tonne truck.

After dinner, Marc rose to rinse the bowls and I followed.

He said, 'I suppose I should look in on her,' meaning the baby, and this is literally what he did. He leaned against the doorjamb, skinny arms folded across his chest, and looked.

'Is she ok?' I whispered.

'Fine,' he said.

'Well, goodnight I guess,' I said. I went to my room.

I have had too many soft knocks on my door to be surprised by soft knocks. I was glad that he did not invent some kind of pretext to come in. I put my phone down, and he went to the lit candle. I thought he would blow it out. Instead, he pinched it between his thumb and forefinger. His belt buckle was level with my eyes.

My vision adjusted to the dark. Soon the light seemed white-blue in that room. I remember being surprised at how thick and impenetrable the bush of his pubic hair turned out to be. I remember tasting chicory on his breath.

Afterwards he stood and said, 'Would you mind getting up?'

I was lying there waiting for him to turn away so I could reach for my bra and make my exit to the bathroom.

'What?'

'Could you just get up please?'

He switched the light on. He put on his trousers. I put an arm over my breasts.

'Can I have my bra?'

He found it and passed it to me, dangling it from one outstretched finger.

I stood. What was on and in me started rolling downwards.

He started stripping the sheets from the bed.

'What are you doing?'

'This mattress is new,' he said. 'There's no protector.'

He pulled the sheets back and looked with revulsion at the colourless stain at the centre of the mattress. He left the room, and returned with the vinegar and baking soda they used to clean everything in that house, along with a child's tiny toothbrush. He brushed fussily for a couple of minutes, then bundled the sheets in his arms.

'You should maybe sleep on the couch tonight,' he said.

I lay on that couch and heard the washing machine gurgle and churn. Beneath that I could hear things moving, outside, through the darkness.

The next day I was woken by the sound of Marc dragging the mattress down the stairs.

'Would you mind?' he asked.

I helped him drag the thing into the garden.

'Sunlight is the best thing,' he said.

Upstairs Lee started crying.

'I'm going to take the baby out,' I said.

This time I went beyond the street. I followed the path into the trees. It didn't seem so wild once you were among them. The silver foil of chip packets glinted in the grass. The bins were studded with wads of gum.

October could still be a cool month in those hills. It was warm in the sunlight, but as we followed the path, moving deeper into the shade of the trees, the baby must have sensed a drop in temperature, must have sensed the blocking of the light.

She started fussing. Then she took one of those huge inhales that meant she was going to scream. For some reason, though I had spent so many weeks listening to her screams, this time it was impossible to endure them. This presented itself to me as a fact: I couldn't tolerate them any longer. I needed to make them stop.

Please understand that the baby survived. I hardly hurt her. I didn't hit her or shake her.

Please understand that everyone left alone with a small child has wondered what they might get away with.

All I did was reach into the pram and pinch her tiny nose shut.

For how long?

Say two seconds?

Say five at the most.

There was sudden quiet. I watched the wrappers flapping in the breeze. I heard the sweep-rush and scrape of leaves flittering along the bitumen.

When I let go she looked at me like she was really looking at me, like she could recognise me.

'Let's go home,' I said.

The weather started to feel more like spring. The sun was brighter, harsher. I would sit by the window while Lee slept and watch my arms turn pink.

Soon her mother would return.

It took me too long to give up on the hope that Marc would come and visit me in the nun's room again. I only let go of the fantasy after one day when I walked into the bathroom and saw him there with the little chrome bin balanced on the sink. He had an expression on his face like he had just broken in through the window.

'Hi,' he said.

There was something in his hand.

I'd seen that look, the look of a guilty man caught unawares. Maya's apartment was empty by the time Cameron came by. I'd opened the door and walked in on him.

We'd stood staring at each other.

Cameron had moved first. He began to inspect the place while I watched. He touched everything, knocking on walls and running his hand along the window sills, checking his fingertips for dust.

'There's nothing here,' I finally said.

He came over to the doorway where I stood. He kept walking until he was only an inch or two away. I stepped back, crossed my arms.

'I was just looking,' he said. 'No harm in looking, is there?'

I stared hard at Marc's hand. I hadn't emptied the bin in a week. I had wrapped my tampons in toilet paper, tightly, like they were bodies that needed to be shrouded for burial. He hadn't asked about birth control, so I suppose he was relieved to unroll one of the little packages and see the evidence of his own safety.

I still remember his wide startled eyes. I can see the little string, brown with old blood, trailing from his closed fist.

A few days before my time in the hills would end, I heard a bang. I looked up and so did the baby.

I ran up the stairs. When I got to the top I saw that Marc had reached

26

the nun's room before I could.

I walked in behind him.

'Oh my god,' I said.

The candle I'd bought had exploded. There was broken glass, a spattering of white wax hardening onto the floor and walls.

When we came closer I saw that it had left a black shadow in the shape of a small spiny cloud – a cartoonish *bang!* – on the drawers' smooth white surface.

Marc didn't say anything, just ran his fingers back and forth through his hair.

'I'll clean this up,' I said. 'I'll pay for any damage.'

'It's fine,' he said. 'Don't worry about it.'

He left the room and came back with a plastic bag, and together we picked up the shards of glass.

'You let it burn down too far,' he said.

'I'm so sorry,' I said.

'It's fine.'

I let the silence stretch for a moment while we placed smaller and smaller shards of glass into the plastic bag. But then I couldn't stop myself. I said, 'I could have burned your house down.'

Our goodbyes were perfunctory. Marc paid me exactly what was owed and I patted Lee on the head, sure that she would have no recollection of me whatsoever.

I saw him working before I left. It was in the morning, before the sun was high and relentless. He had taken the chest of drawers into the garden and was sanding it, removing the white paint to show the raw timber underneath.

I peered down from my window, focusing all the energy of my gaze into his bald spot, which gleamed with perspiration as he worked. It was the unlikely hot pink of a baby mouse. I was high enough to get a good, clear view of his thin body worrying at its task. I'm not sure whether he could sense me looking, feel the ferocity of my concentration. If he did see me, he gave no indication. For a moment this saddened me.

But then I thought that it was probably for the best. Yes, I thought. The best thing would be if he couldn't see me at all. The best thing would be if he never saw me again.

3rd Prize
Helen Rye

Helen Rye lives in Norwich, UK. Her short stories have won the Bath Flash Fiction Award, the Reflex Fiction Prize, been shortlisted for the Bridport Prize and nominated for Best Small Fictions 2017 and 2018. She is a submissions editor at SmokeLong Quarterly and a fiction editor for Lighthouse Literary Journal, and part of the Ellipsis Zine editorial board.

Transposition

Ahab sets the carved chessmen out on the board in the department store window. An unfinished game. His fingers hold the muscle memory of each position. The image of every chess piece is burnt into his mind. He sees them in the streets at night, in the lines of people's faces, in the dreams he has that make the man in the hostel room next door bang on paper-thin walls in the small hours and shout for him to be quiet.

Sokolsky opening. Pawn to b4.

Expensively dressed dummies surround him, blank eyes staring. The mannequin nearest to him is bent down, peering over his shoulder, watching under the hot display lights as he prepares to take up play.

Bishop to e5. Black castles.

His hands are shaking. He slides them along the chair, under his thighs, tries to still them with his weight, knucklebones against smooth wood.

Plate glass separates him from the people crossing the tiled walkway outside like pawns in another game. None of them are looking at him. Not yet. He wonders what strategies they have to make them move with such purpose.

Knight to f6. Your game is passive, tonight, Ahab, my friend.

The words play across memory again and again, always so clear that he finds it hard to believe he does not hear them spoken aloud, although he tries to hold onto this knowledge - it is the least he can do. So little of the here-and-now remains steady, these days. The fight to stay tethered in the empty present tires him. In the mornings when he goes to the public library, the high ceiling merges with that of a shaded lecture hall half a world away. In the autumn damp of these streets he tastes the desert. He sees the sun-washed stone of that other city, his rooms, the dark stains on the table where he last pored over this board. He remembers their conversation, that night, their moves. He remembers everything.

Your strategy is a little off, here, I think.

I am happy with my position. You must worry about this knight. Or do you choose to lose your bishop?

Eyes flickering in the candlelight, laughing. Ahab can smell the hot wax.

Bishop to e2.

Across the table, in his mind, he sees Rami.

Rami. Slight, quiet, broken by years of living in a city under siege, his body branded with scars that mapped the deeper ones inside his head. Rami, who could no longer walk in the street after dark, who cradled himself into a foetal curl under his desk when a car backfired. Rami, who could see ten moves ahead in a game, hold possibilities in his mind that Ahab couldn't guess at. Rami, whose quick smile came rarely but made Ahab feel the ground beneath him slip, the two of them together, falling.

Bishop to g4. Ahab's move. He speaks as he lifts the chess piece, concentrating on placing it accurately so that he will not have to look Rami in the face.

They will never stop until we are all dead, Rami. All of us. Academics, teachers, doctors. All of us.

Pawn to c4.

You know this is true.

Queen to b3.

The end of Rami's cigarette glows. He breathes out long, studies the board.

Ahab persists.

Come with me. I have a little money. We can go to Europe, make a new start. We can do it. Together.

White castles. Rami looks up at last.

I cannot. You know this.

Knight to a3.

I know that I want you to come with me.

I cannot leave my homeland. The cells of my body were made from the dust here. What else is there? I cannot even go out in the dark. I would rather stay and die in my own city than live as a stranger in a land that does not know me.

Rook to - rook to -

What else is there?

Ahab picks up the rook, turns it over in his hand, sets it back down.

You know what else, Rami. You know. But. If you really -

He gets up, turns his back on Rami, walks over to the tiny kitchen, and this is when it happens, the banging on the door, the near-simultaneous crash, the shouting, and Ahab is inside a cupboard hiding before he knows what he is doing and he hears Rami's voice, crying, saying there is nobody else here, there is nobody, and then five shots, so loud that Ahab can hear nothing more, for the seconds or minutes or days it takes for his body to unfold itself, but his own heart pounding, pounding, his own pulse freight-train loud in his ears. Then he runs, runs to find Rami alone on the floor and his blood spread over everything Ahab has ever owned, its metallic smell, and somewhere there is a sound like a fox screaming, and it is a while before Ahab realises that it is coming from his own mouth.

And now Ahab is here, in this new land, this unfamiliar place that fades from his mind like a ghost city, where none of his cells belong, and there is banging on the door of the department store display, but he has wedged a chair under the handle, and people are gathering outside the glass, now, watching him, watching the foreign man with the chessboard, weeping silently in a shop window.

He shuts his eyes, and the world shrinks down to black and white, until there are only squares and chess pieces. Order and logic. He runs potential moves over in his mind, sees how the game might unfold, strategies he'd thought forgotten playing out with cinematic realism. He touches lightly each piece in its turn in the litany, each move flowing from the last and foreshadowing the next.

Pawn takes knight, and Ahab has the advantage, but he doesn't want to take it, and now there is constant hammering on the door and shouting, the sound of heavy boots running, and people are being driven back from the window, and he will not hide, this brown man barricaded in the western shopping mall. He knows what will come, and he will not hide.

He allows *bishop to b5* and does not act; sacrifices his knight, his queen. Lays down his king in surrender and hands the game to Rami, to his cells that lie in the dust of home, to what else there could have been.

3rd Prize
Zeus Sumra

Zeus Sumra was born and raised in Saint Lucia. He emigrated to the United States when he was 17. Recently, he graduated with a BA in Psychology from Brooklyn College where he served as a Managing News Editor for the Kingsman Newspaper. As an undergraduate, Zeus won many awards for his short stories including 1st prize for both The Goodman Short Story Award and The Bertha and Philip Goodman Short Story Award and 2nd prize in the City University of New York Labor Arts contest. He lives in Westchester, NY where he writes about West Indians at home and abroad.

Little Yellow Planes

Months before, the gooseberries fell in abundance. The citric paste that formed on the outsoles of our sandals smelled like sweet decay. All the pawpaw plants drooped with heavy, amber fruits. The afternoon breeze cooled our skin and emptied the air of stifling moisture.

But now, the trees stuck out thirstily from the parched ground. Everything smelled like nothing. The leaves of the mango trees had a paper-like texture, and we waited in vain for fresh, soft buds to appear. Even the banana blades – some green, others yellowing – were now dotted with brown spots. Thankfully, *pommecythere* trees, no matter how their dehydrated leaves curled in on themselves or how grainy the soil turned, had branches that stretched out like muscled arms. It was on one of those branches that Anita made a swing with nylon webbing, the ones her father used to secure boxes of bananas on the pickup truck, and tied it to wooden planks for Katy and me.

I swung back-and-forth. Katy swung forward and then back. Anita stood between the two swings, guiding our movements. We admired Anita for her creativity. She was the one who came up with the idea to use the dried palm fronds, peeled them, and harvested the thin twigs. We built a tiny house with them. She also came up with the idea to use the skirting polymer bags from her father's shed, a whole bunch of them, wound up to form a ball to play *rounders*. Katy and I threw the ball to each other, Anita ran cunningly between us, dodging our every attempt to strike her out. There were also the times she did things I thought were cruel. Like the time she poured rubbing alcohol over an anthill to see what the queen ant looked like. I was silent about that. Better than being bored, I told Katy. Despite all the great ideas she came up with, though she was in Standard Four, and I in Standard Two, I always had to help her with her home work. She couldn't name the capitals of other islands, couldn't spell February correctly and had trouble computing long division questions with remainders in the answer. Once, she had to stand out in the school compound at midday, with her hands raised above her shoulders. Her face had displayed a sneaky indifference, her lips slightly stretched almost to a grin as if she wasn't close to collapsing from sunstroke. Later that day, she told me that it was because she had gotten all the questions wrong when the teacher quizzed her class on the multiplication table. Anita knew tricks and ideas, grown-up things too, just not a thing that would help her pass her examinations.

It was while Katy and I were swinging from the *pommecythere* tree that Anita told us about the war. "Didn't you hear? They said a new World War is happening soon, and, it might come here."

I asked her where she had heard these things, and, why she would tell us such lies.

"Do you have television at your home to watch news?" she said, tugging at the fat of her earlobe and then laughed. "I am telling you. I saw it on the news last night. My parents were talking about it. My father said they no longer even use bombs these days; they use this new thing called chemical weapons. Those big, big countries just send little planes to spray over the place and the people, animals, trees – everything just die like that." She snapped her finger in our faces as she finished making that last claim.

"Liar!" Katy turned her face, flushed with concern, away from Anita.

Anita slowly shook her head, with a sorry look on her face. "I'm only telling you the truth. All the trees will slowly die and we won't have food. And then, everyone will have foam coming out of their mouth as if we had swallowed *Breeze* soap powder." She clasped her throat with both hands while saying this, her head made epileptic movements, her mouth wide-open. Her whole body shivered and then she collapsed into growing laughter.

I asked Anita to stop telling us these things. I told her that she was making Katy – who by then was already crying – feel scared. I, too, was uneasy. Before she left, she put on a malevolent smirk and said, "Just wait and see."

Daddy came shortly after. I saw him from afar, holding up two drunk men and another stammering behind. They were all workers on Anita's father, Mr. Richie's, banana farm. He winked at us, walked up the hill to take them to their respective houses and then came home. This was their Friday night ritual. Most of the men spent the small wages that they earned from working the farm at the bar. They drank themselves into a stupor. Daddy did not drink, he usually sat on the stoop of the bar shelling peanuts. That was what he smelled like when he finally got home. It was what he smelled like every Friday night. With a tired look in his eyes, he asked me what had happened today. I told him about school, I told him about our new swing under the *pommecythere* tree, but I did not tell him what Anita told us – at least not yet.

I thought that he might get upset at Anita and ask her to stop coming to our house. And Katy and I wanted Anita to come back, to teach us some new trick. Our enjoyment hinged on her inventiveness. We simply didn't want her to tell us about war planes and death.

Often, daddy told us stories. They always began with him saying, "*il dit qui!*" And we responded with, "*quoi?*" I didn't know what it meant then. I had asked him, but, often, he responded with a look that said, you shouldn't question adults. Or he would tell us that it was how his mother taught him to tell a story, and that was also how his grandmother had taught his mother. He told us stories of *Anansi* the spider, *Daddy-longlegs* and the harvestman, and *Compère Lapin*, the rabbit. His rich French-Creole accent added energy to the stories. But I could see all the energy was sucked out of him from the work-week, so I didn't bother asking him to tell me a story then.

For days after, when we saw Anita walking to school, she would dance her way ahead of us and giggle in a mildly deranged manner as if to say, "Just wait. Just wait."

It happened just like that, while Katy and I were on the swings under the *pommecythere* tree. Anita had not visited us since, and, we were being too stubborn to take turns to push each other on the swings, so we tilted the plank seats of the swings forward for momentum. When the sound of the planes overhead came, Katy fell head-first onto the ground. Loud vibrations thundered above us and sent waves of worry through me. I had to pull Katy to my core. She screamed and then curled herself up into a shell. When the sound had faded to silence, I lifted her up. Tears streamed down her cheeks faster than I could wipe them off with my fearful fingers. I cradled her like a baby until her sobs started to die down then began telling her a story.

Il dit qui!

quoi?

There was a little girl who lived with her mother. They were very poor, and so, the house they lived in was infested with insects: spiders, caterpillars, roaches. She was most afraid of the caterpillars with their stumpy legs. At night, she wept until her mother sang a cradlesong that made her drowsy enough for her eyes to close. One night, the mother's singing did not do the trick. No matter what song the mother tried, the little girl kept on crying remembering a caterpillar she had spotted while they were having supper. So, the mother made her tea with soursop leaves that made her very drowsy. The girl's mother wrapped her around and around in her bedsheets and whispered: "sleep, you will never be afraid of caterpillars again." The following morning, when the girl woke up, she had brilliant blue wings like a butterfly.

When I was done telling the story, Katy no longer took quick breaths. She inhaled calmly, as if my storytelling had made the air fresher, more comforting. She still trembled a little when I took her into the house. I made her tea with soursop leaves. After she drank the tea, I told her to lay down until she fell asleep, and that when she woke up she would no longer be afraid of the little yellow planes.

No sooner than Katy was in bed, mommy came home from working at Mr. Richie's farm where she washed the bananas in a sulfate bath before boxing them, and, she also prepared food for all the workers to eat at the end of the day. As the bananas became less and less in the drought, she also helped Mr. Richie and the men to cover the hanging clusters with skirting polymer bags and added manure to the soil. She looked more hunched than before and her feet dragged lazily to her room. She told me to hurry and finish my homework so that I could get enough sleep. I was used to staying up so late and alone doing homework. Katy didn't have many homework assignments because she was still in Mr. Peters' Stage-Three class. Mr. Peters also taught me lessons after school. Daddy had paid for them, though, I knew, he could barely afford them. Mommy tried to convince him not to. She reasoned that I was consistently ranking first in class, but, daddy said that he did not just want me to be first in class when

I took Mock Exams at the end of the year. He wanted me to rank first in the entire district. Anita had big exams coming up at the end of the school term as well. She was taking the Common Entrance Exam that would determine if she attended one of the local Secondary schools in the district or one of those big Catholic Secondary schools in the city. Though Mr. Richie owned the farm, and unlike daddy, could afford lessons, Antia did not enroll in private lessons.

Our house had no electricity, so I sat with a kerosene oil lamp at the desk my father had made – three slabs of beach wood supported by four bamboo stalks. Shortly after, I heard the laughter of the drunken workers approaching, so I expected daddy to walk in at any moment. He came in shortly after and smiled gently in the direction of me working at the desk, revealing a thin layer of brown seed coat glued to his front teeth. I couldn't tell whether he was pleased with me studying or the desk that he had made until he felt his own callused hand through my hair and said that he was proud of me. I wanted to tell him that Katy and I were afraid of staying at home by ourselves after school, that Anita no longer came by to keep us company, and that we were so afraid of the yellow planes. But I didn't.

It became an event to expect on Fridays: the little yellow planes. Katy bowed down, cradling in on me so that when she cried my dress became drenched with her tears. Once, I got the courage to look up and I saw one of the planes, it looked like a low-flying kite. It glided over the village spraying a white fog everywhere, similar to when mommy sprayed Baygon at sundown so that we would not get bit by mosquitoes. Cottons of smoke marked its trail. Sometimes, it passed over an area twice as if to make sure that the white fog had covered the place. When it passed near us again, Katy's squeals were louder; I tried to rub her back in that same caressing way that mommy circled Vicks Vaporub on our chest when we had a cold.

The plane flew so low that I saw the pilot in the cockpit, a fierce, dark face with squinting eyes, and I felt as though if I jumped high enough I could touch the bottom of the plane. It looked as if the plane would fly straight into a cashew tree but the pilot made a sudden lift of the nose, and rocketed upwards until the sound, once loud, became a whispering hum fading into our scarred memories.

"It's okay now *Bubu*," I said. Sometimes, I called Katy *Bubu* because it reminded her of the times we played house. Katy always played the baby, and, I, the mother who was supposed to protect her from the wicked witch, Anita. I felt my lips moving to tell Katy a story in that same mothering manner.

Il dit qui!

quoi?

On an island, there was a settlement near a lake. A young man there liked his settlement but he was frustrated about the fruits that grew there. All the various fruits bloomed with abundance when in season, and like a magic trick, they also disappeared at the same time in off-season. So, he paid a fisherman to take him on the lake, hoping to find another settlement with crops that bore fruit during his own settlement's off-season. When he arrived at the new settlement across the lake, he asked to view their crops. Upon looking, the man was very disappointed. The crops were the same as the ones in his settlement. When he shared his hope of finding different crops, the chief told him, you will have to go to another island to find new crops. To get to the next island, you have to first get to the beach and then sail to the horizon. But be careful. Some who sail to the horizon never come back. Some come back, but are never the same.

Katy's crying lowered to a soft moan but she was still trembling, and after I offered to make her tea she said that she did not want it because the tea didn't make her less afraid of the planes. She went back to sobbing and screaming with drool trickling from the corners of her lips. The more she cried, the more fear I felt and it took a while to collect myself but then I started toward the bar. The bar smelled like smoke, wet cigarette buds and suffocating alcohol, all at once. Daddy asked me why Katy was crying and I told him. He walked us over to Mr. Richie's house, he called Anita outside and told her to tell us the truth. Anita told us that the little yellow planes were not war planes. Their emissions were not chemicals that could kill us, but pesticides. And she even scolded us. "Don't you see that's why the banana leaves have brown spots?"

My father raised his hand over his left shoulder as if to strike her with the back of his hand, but held it firm in mid-air. "Shut your mouth, stupid girl. Don't you see they are small girls, children in fact, and that they will believe anything? Is that reason to scare them this way?"

Anita was silent. Then my father said the words I feared he would say, the words that poured concrete over my fears and made them permanent, "Don't come to my house anymore." The way her eyes were dead, and her nostrils opened wide with each inhalation, I knew she would never speak to us again after this.

The following Friday, the little yellow planes came. Katy and I sat on the *pommecythere* swings and we watched the planes for the first time together, without fear. We curled our hands into binoculars and squinted at the planes as they moved in the same way when I had looked the last time. I thought to myself that maybe these planes follow some invisible route, or maybe invisible to us, but the pilots could definitely see it. Our binoculars shifted in a vertical plane following every movement. They swooshed up and down, fell low and tilted with precise angles. And then the humming faded, silence came and brought boredom with it. Katy fell asleep that night without me telling her a story or making her soursop tea. That was the last time we saw the little yellow planes.

Things were different after that. Exam time neared, and daddy increased my lessons from one hour after school with Mr. Peters to three. Katy would wait for me during the entire lesson, and by the time the two of us reached home, it was time to wash the dust off our feet. Katy and I had dinner, dry loaves and Milo without milk. I stayed up studying at the Bamboo-and-Beachwood desk while Katy slept. The men came to our house now instead of going to the bar. Mr. Richie had not called anyone to help on the farm for weeks, and they assembled to complain about how the banana plants were drooping and dying, that there was no more work, and the fact that Mr. Richie had not paid them their final wages. Sometimes, one of the men would bring a home-made spiced rum, and they would get drunk. They used foul language when they joked around. They laughed and spat and sometimes, fought – they became different, alive.

My mother did not like the men coming. She, too, was out of work and the gloominess she bore when she came home tired from work was more common. She smiled, however, when I brought my report book home. I had not only placed first in the school, but in the district. Mommy prepared roasted breadfruit and smoked herring for us to celebrate, and in that moment it seemed as if she had gained back all her youth. "We finally got paid today," she said, and lit up.

Daddy smiled, too, but he didn't exactly light up and look like his old self. He just sat there, chewing the breadfruit and swallowing very thoughtfully. "We still don't know where the money will come when you do your Common Entrance to go to Secondary School in the city." Thin lines of worry spread across his copper skin

"We have two years to figure that out," mommy said, smiling through a mouthful of breadfruit. The honey-brown skin of her cheeks bulged, resembling the pufferfish on the cover of my *Macmillan Caribbean School Atlas*. That made Katy and I laugh out loud, until we were coughing from our full stomachs.

"But what about that Anita? Did she pass her exams?" mommy asked.

I told mommy that Anita had not passed at all, and that she might be repeating Standard Four. It was what one of the students in her class had told me. Mommy shook her head. Daddy didn't say anything, his face expressionless as if this was not news, he expected no different.

Later that day, I heard laughter coming up from the hill. Daddy had left after we celebrated the family lunch. Through the louvres, I saw the workers approaching. Daddy did not help the other men up the steps. He walked unsteadily like all the men. They swayed and bumped, grabbing onto each others' shoulder for support. One of the men fell on the lawn and I thought that he would remain there until the next day, but, the other men made fun of him and eventually helped him up so that they could climb the hill together. Daddy came in, his smile nearly reaching the dimple in his cheeks. He kept on laughing and calling me *Bubu*. "*Bubu*, my girl," he kept on saying. Mommy sucked her teeth and told me to put my books away and go to my room. She didn't argue but I could sense her rage. The air felt stifling that night. It took me hours after daddy quietened to fall asleep.

In the morning, a fresh breeze filtered through the bedroom rousing Katy and me from sleep. A strong clean scent of Clorox irritated my nostrils. All the louvres and doors were opened, the floor still damp from being mopped. I thought daddy would be fast asleep, still drunk from the night before, but he was no where in sight.

"Come," mommy said. "Your father picked all the last of the *pommecythere* this morning. Help me hold this." She handed Katy and me, each, one edge of a tank top with the fruit pulp. She poured a jug of water over it, and we listened to the soft sound of the diluted liquid accumulate in the bowl, interrupted only by the rubbery sound of tires coming up the hill.

Through the kitchen louvres, I saw the white car pull up in front of Anita's house, and shortly after, she appeared very well-dressed in bright blue jeans and a long sleeve shirt that looked too warm for the late morning heat. Behind her, her parents lugged two suit cases. Mr. Richie smiling, her mother's face was big and round with sadness.

I felt a hand grab at my arm so forcefully, that a rush of adrenaline brought my body into a little shock. It was my father, he pushed Katy and I into the couch. "Don't you two have to study?" He spoke with such force that Katy snivelled.

"Eugene, you can at least let them say good bye to Anita before she catches her flight."

"Don't they have studying to do?" The skin of his face was firmer, the muscles collecting into a fixed rage. "Do their parents have money to send them to private schools abroad?"

We sat at the desk in a long and uncomfortable silence. I kept on reading the same sentence over and over, I didn't understand a word of what I was reading. Then, daddy got up and carried Katy with one of his strong arms, placed her to his side and padded the settee cushion next to him for me to sit.

"*Il dit qui,*" he started.

I was nervous, but I still managed to speak with a shaky voice. "But daddy, you have not told us what that phrase means."

"Listen," he said with his index finger pressed against his lips.

Il dit qui!

quoi?

When we were young, our mothers and fathers told stories to us at bedtime. It was not uncommon to have nothing to eat for dinner and so, our bellies would grumble. The storyteller would say out loud: It is said that! And we reply even louder: What? They begin a story that way so that our mind is in the story.

Not for us to hear, but for us to listen. Our eyes would strain at the moving lips, our bodies become light, ready to be transported. When the story was finished being told, you would not remember that your belly was empty. You would go to bed dreaming.

Aniqah Choudhri

Aniqah Choudhri works for an international charity and is a theatre critic for Exeunt Magazine. She has just come third in the Hippocrates Prize for Poetry and Medicine 2018. She won the Lightship Flash Fiction Prize in 2013 and is working on a novel. She lives in Manchester and takes a lot of inspiration for her writing from the gothic and windswept countryside of the Peak District. She tweets at @aniqahc and has an Instagram devoted to books at @aniqahreads

Chicken Heart

A fox has broken into the coop and dragged out a chicken. Its tawny muzzle is wet with blood as it tears into the soft, fat little body.

"Nooo," moans Habiba, "Feo go and stop him."

Feo doesn't say anything. The fox is crunching the bones now, chewing voraciously at the fatty ends. Her husband is unnaturally still next to her and the only light is the moon glowing like a paper lantern through the glass. She feels a cold thrill run through her.

"Make sure I'm buried within 24 hours," Habiba says suddenly, unable to help herself. Her voice quavers and dies like that of a rabbit caught in a trap.

Feo looks at her then. "Darling," he says tenderly.

He makes her chamomile tea and puts her to bed. He smells of fir sap and frankincense and she dreams of a great gold incense burner ticking like a grandfather clock.

It is Midsummer and the grass is burnt gold and crackling.

When Habiba stumps out to get eggs in the morning the hens cluck around her, warm and contented. She likes the way they follow in a line when she feeds them, leading them back to their coop. The basket in the kitchen is full of warm eggs, living and smooth. She boils one for breakfast and eats it with tea warm from the samovar.

In the afternoon she hears a woman's cry from the spare room and pointedly slams the bathroom door as she bleaches the toilet. There is a crack like the snapping of a tree branch and then silence.

Feo brings glasses after glass after glass of cool water in the evening and watches to make sure she drinks them. Habiba wonders if he's waiting for the water to fill her up like a balloon, smoothing all her wrinkles out and making her hair silk not straw.

"Your moustache has grown back again," he says one night as she watches a lacklustre episode of Coronation Street. "I don't like it."

"You can shave it off if you don't disturb me," says Habiba.

He wets her face with a damp cloth and then softly scrapes the razor across it, careful of her wrinkles.

"Do we have to watch this?"

"It's not a very good episode. I'm going to bed soon."

"Stay up for a bit. I've barely seen you." He's wearing a new jumper with NASA written on it. He dresses much more casually now they stay at home. She thinks sometimes he goes out when she's asleep but she's not sure. It is night when she can feel Death standing over her, his breath rattling in her face. She is sure if Feo were there he would never let him in the room.

The care worker this week is a man in his fifties. He is built solidly like a woodcutter and has strong brown arms and a big black beard.

"Does your grandson like NASA podcasts?" he says looking at Feo's jumper as he checks her pulse. "My son loves them."

He talks in that extra loud friendly voice that people use with very old people or to children. Feo sits scowling in the armchair opposite them. Habiba knows from her mirror this morning that her spine is curved like a fishing hook, her hair is as thin as spiderwebs and her face is drooping like halva off a spoon.

"Now that's enough of that," Habiba croaks to Feo in Punjabi when the man starts to look uncomfortable as he shows her how to exercise her creaking joints.

"Where are you from Aunty?" the man says.

"Lahore," says Habiba. She had come over on a boat when she was five. She only remembered holding her mother's hand and seeing the seagulls tearing each other apart in the sky.

"My parents are from Islamabad," the man says. He's waiting for her to ask further, to reminisce about the old country but she doesn't care enough. Feo ends up filling in for her, making small talk while she drifts briefly. He keeps holding his hands purposely in front of him so the wedding ring is visible. Habiba doesn't have the heart to tell him the idea that they could be married would never cross this man's mind even if he came over and kissed her full on the lips.

Sometimes Feo takes her out to eat although he obsessively reads the food hygiene rating for each place after she got food poisoning from a newly opened Afghan restaurant. She likes it best when he takes her for Russian and they both ignore the anxious waiting staff as he solicitously pours her glass after glass of vodka and feeds her flaky sugary baklava and spoons of borscht. Her body doesn't react well to this decadence as they discover.

"I think you've wet yourself again," Feo hisses in her ear over the clink of cutlery and tasteful classical music. Every part of him is stiff with embarrassment.

"What?" barks Habiba purely to annoy him, "I can't hear you, speak louder."

Mostly they stay at home and he makes dahl and fluffy bowls of rice and cuts her apple pieces with the skin peeled. She likes it best when they can sit in the garden in the early evening and hear the buzz of the insects and watch the sky darkening. He seems to enjoy it too, he goes along with whatever she likes these days, but he must be restless. Sometimes he talks about the past, their past not his, and she is happy to join in with this.

"Do you remember when we first met?" he says one evening. "You were wringing a chicken's neck for Eid. The blood was dripping in the gutter."

"That never happened," says Habiba. "We've done this. You must be thinking of someone else."

He looks at her clearly irritated.

"I never killed a chicken. I saw someone do it once and I felt sick."

"If you say so," Feo says, neutral. "It's late now, lets go to sleep."

"Yes Grandpa," she wheezes and he looks annoyed and then they both start snickering until she has a hacking fit.

"Don't look so upset," she sighs.

"How would you like me to look?" he asks. He gnashes his teeth and she hears the clang of iron.

She thought about leaving Feo several times but came closest in the winter of 1954.

Every morning she woke up hating the rain sleeting against the narrow window, the griminess of the view outside and the smell of smoke and cheap scent on his suit crumpled over the hard wooden chair.

One night he comes home and she still hasn't gone to bed. He takes off his damp coat and hangs it by the door then comes over to where she is smoking at the window.

"I don't like you having the windows open at night."

She shrugs. The record player is hissing in the background as it reaches the end of the track. "Did you have a nice tea?"

He draws in a deep breath but then lets it out and smiles tightly. "It was fine." He leans over and shuts the window.

"Oh leave it open it's so stuffy in here."

"What do you expect?" he shakes the saucer she's been using as an ashtray, messy with ash.

He lights up, "I thought smoking was prohibited in The Q'uaran."

Her face heats up and she opens the window with a jerk. "There are different levels of sins."

"Obviously," he drawls.

Later they lie in bed like two planks of wood. She aches with tiredness but can't sleep. When the moon sets he rolls over and puts his face to her neck and she smells the familiar coppery tang that makes her heart lurch before he bites.

She stays in bed late the next morning and imagines waking up in a different bed, in a different city. She finally drags herself up, eyes puffy, and sees Feo sitting in the chair by the window. He was so quiet she didn't even sense him in the room. He's holding a crumpled letter in his hand, she recognises the writing on the address and her heart stops.

"What's this?" he says quietly.

The fight that follows is so loud the woman who lives in the flat downstairs, an Irish woman who Habiba nods to on the stairs, starts banging her ceiling and yells they've woken her baby up.

Feo can't storm out, its daytime, so she does and she takes the letter with her, more importantly what's inside. If he knew he would never let her leave. She opens it on the bus and stares at the train ticket and then at the last lines her sister has written We'll sort it out when you get here. They'll forgive you when they see you. I miss you.

She sits at Piccadilly station all day. Drinks cup after cup of tea. At 4:30

a woman with a pram struggles to push by her and she moves her chair and smiles at the little girl walking behind.

"Come on madam," the woman says as the girl dawdles. She doesn't acknowledge Habiba.

"How old is she?" Habiba asks

The woman looks at her, her face impassive, and moves on.

Habiba sits back down. All the energy has left her. She doesn't know if she can make it back to the flat let alone to Glasgow.

She thinks of the house full of cousins, and aunts and uncles, and her sister, and the dahl and roti that will be cooking this evening, maybe even nihari, tender pieces of lamb simmering all day over the stove, fluffy white rice and tea around the table after. Watching their mouths chew and swallow the food, mouthful after mouthful instead of eating alone night after night.

She uses the last of her money on the new copy of *The Junior Astronomer* and takes the bus home.

She sits at the little kitchen table when she gets in not even bothering to see if Feo is there. He comes up behind her.

"I got this for you," Feo says.

He places a pomegranate on a plate in front of her, already cut in half. The seeds glisten red, in their honeycomb like pattern, brighter than anything in the flat. She picks up one half and bites into it while Feo scrapes the seeds out of the other. It's sweet and tart.

Feo heats water for a steaming bath and she lights candles in the window until she is bathing in hot light and water. A fox screams outside and Feo knocks on the door and says he has had dinner and what would she like? He'll make anything. Habiba thinks of him chewing into his dinner outside in the bitter smoky air and calls through the door. When she emerges he has a hot meat pie that flakes when she cuts it open and is filled with tender lamb and thick rich gravy.

She leaves a large white candle burning in the window to ward off evil against the iced over sky.

They have come across acquaintances of Feo a few times.

They had been walking to the river. It is a week after Habiba's hip operation and she walks leaning heavily on his arm when a man in a dark wool coat says disbelievingly "Feodor? Feodor Vladamitvitch?"

Feo tenses then like he is planning on walking on then thinks better of it. The man is dark, handsome, stockier than Feo and taller. His red rimmed eyes flicker over Habiba without taking her in and then to Feo and a slow smile is spreading across his face that makes Habiba look away.

"What are you doing?" the man says. "*Here?*" He laughs, a rough bark, and reaches out to touch Feo's shoulder. Feo doesn't move but his face twitches.

The man doesn't seem to notice. "It's been so long. Not since – ," his eyes flicker to Habiba again and then switches to Russian.

"Not since the summer at Kislovodsk" the man says. "I was so angry when you left that morning but I understand now." His breath comes out in a sigh. "So much has happened since then. Where can we go? I've only been here a few days."

Habiba might be a dog Feo is taking for a walk for all the attention this man is paying to her. Only the warning grip Feo has on her arm keeps her from saying anything. His face is pleasant, open. He's staring towards this man but his eyes are glazed like he's calculating several possibilities out in his mind and none of them sound appealing.

"I can't go anywhere right now," Feo says pleasantly. "Why don't you give me your number and I'll call you."

"Oh just go," says Habiba unable to help herself. Feo's arm stiffens.

The man looks at her then, properly for the first time, sizing her up but Feo suddenly comes to life drawing the attention back to him.

"Liosha," he says warmly, "lets go for a drink tomorrow. Where are you staying? I'll go there."

They part from the man and walk towards the station and Feo is still walking slowly and considerately for her. People who see them smile seeing a young man taking his grandmother for a stroll. Habiba's mouth is shaking uncontrollably. She can't see where they're going.

Feo says, "I have to go. Otherwise he'll come sniffing around the house."

"I can't stop you," Habiba chokes. She wishes she didn't need his arm to lean on to walk. She wishes she were young again and could storm off, that she weren't as dependent on him as a life support.

"He's not a safe person. If you were – ."

"Oh stop bringing it up." Habiba snarls. "I can't do that! I won't do that. Thats the one thing I won't do!"

Feo is stiff next to her and for one horrible moment she thinks he will walk away and leave her propped against the wall like a parcel but of course he doesn't. They walk in silence all the way home.

On the last day of summer she wakes up and her whole body hurts. She drags open her eyes and Feo is sitting there as animate as the chair underneath him.

"Please," he says.

Habiba laughs but it comes out of her mouth like the caw of a crow. "I can't feel my hands and feet. It takes me an hour to cross from one end of the house to the other. You want to do it now?"

"It was on the news yesterday," Feo says, "a man in Australia got a new heart. We could just... keep replacing it."

Habiba stares at him

Habiba is dreaming. She has just turned 18 and is behind the counter of her family's store. Twilight has just fallen and the stars are glittering.

A man with messy russet hair and a clever lazy face is buying two pounds of tea. She weighs it out for him.

"You buy tea here every day now," she says. "How can one man drink so much tea?"

His eyes, oddly black for his colouring, are roving on the wall behind her and he smiles. "Finally she speaks," he says. "I wondered what your voice sounded like."

"You could have just spoken to me before."

"I wanted to see how long it would take you to recognise me."

"You must have a lot of time to come here everyday just to wait for me to speak first."

"Yes." He pauses, "I do."

A few sandwiches short of a picnic there Habiba thinks.

Habiba wakes up and tries to scream but all that comes out is a grunt. Her chest is aching and her room is swimming before her eyes. Her heart lurches like the frantic wing beats of a hen before the twist and sickening drop.

She sees Feo's face and the pink tears running down it.

"No not yet," he is saying, "not yet."

"Sorry," Habiba tries to say but already she is slipping back into the dream.

Maureen Cullen

Maureen Cullen lives in Argyll & Bute. She has a distinction in MA Creative Writing from Lancaster University. In 2016, she was published, along with three other poets, in *Primers 1*, a collaboration between Nine Arches Press and the Poetry School. Her short fiction won The Labello Prize in 2014, and she has stories shortlisted at Fish Short Story Prize, Exeter Story Prize, Hysteria, Evesham Festival of Words, HISSAC, Ink Tears, The Short Fiction Prize, Wells Festival and Willesden Herald. Maureen recently completed a short story collection and has embarked on her debut novel.

Havoc Shore

Ah bolt up the path, past Deid Man's Cave, past the nuns' school an hame tae hide under the stairs in the dark, tae Tam gets in.

Da bangs the front door, thumps by me, sits doon on his chair an bawls fer his tea on the fuckin table. Ah stink but ah'll no come oot tae Tam gets in.

Da sometimes finds me when ah'm hiding. He shouts, Billy Boy come here tae ah clout ye wan, an pulls me oot like a winkle by ma ear. But the day he cannae be arsed. He curses at oor Betty tae she runs greetin up the stairs. Oor Cathy goes efter her. Ah wish Tam wid get in soon.

Da talks tae hissel. Where's aw the chanty wrastlers an bastards o this toon, gie em tae me... where's ma Molly? How come Christ took her an left me wi soddin fools o weans?

He glugs frae the stone jar he gets the whisky in efter it's been stole frae the Bond. Efter a while, it's dunked on the fireplace. When he's snorin ah run up tae ma bed even though ah've no hid ma tea.

Ah goes tae sleep but wakes up. There's bootsteps on the stairs. Ah peek oot. Tam carries oor Betty past ma door, her arms roon his neck, her feet danglin. He shooshes her quiet. He says, it's awright, ah've got ye noo. There's a stink o Da's whisky an his smoke aboot her. Her nightie's tore. The lacy bit hangs doon. Tam's shakin wi the cauld.

He goes intae the lassies' room an ah wait at the door. He lies her doon, covers her up an pits Dolly on the pilla. When he comes oot ah asks him fer a piece. He jist looks at the wall behind me, his face aw crumpled like when he lifted Ma's coffin. Ah tug his jacket an he breathes oot so hard he blows his fringe up frae his forehead. He says, don't go doon the stairs, ah'll bring it up.

But he must've forgot cause he disnae come back.

Ah bum doon the stairs an poke ma nose intae the livin room. The lamp's on, there's big shadows ower the walls. Da's oot fer the coont on his chair. His heid's aw squinty, leanin back, an his eyelids ur like the wings on they dyin flies.

Ah jump when Tam says, Billy boy get back tae yer bed.

But Tam, ah'm starvin.

Da's heid's aw wet. Shiny, like oil's goin doon his hair intae his ear.

Tam says, he's fell an knocked hissel.

Better get the doctor?

The fire spits an ah jumps mare.

Tam says, nae need. Go get a piece an some milk an go back tae yer bed. Ah'll sit wi him.

Ah goes past Da. His throat creaks. He's aw grey even wi the fire on full bung. Tam says, get on Billy. So ah goes tae the kitchen, switches on the light, takes oot the jam, spreads it on ma piece, bends it so it sticks, gets ma milk an goes past em agin. The scar on Tam's cheek's like butcher's string. He stares at Da like he'd bash him if he moved. The jug aside Da's chair's aw gooey red.

Tam's bashed him awready.

That's how he cannae be goin fer the doctor.

Da's gone quiet.

Ginger's bed's empty.

Ah spill ma milk ower ma haun. Tam looks at the cat's box an shakes his heid. He says, she's lookin fer her kittens. He gets up, takes ma cup an ma elba, helps me up the stairs. At the top he says, ye saw nothin here the night, understand?

Ah nod, ah unnerston awright.

Ma says, clear the decks, quick noo, afore Da comes. Clear the decks or it'll be a skelp on the arse. The plates ur washed an the shoes ur polished an the weans ur tae shut up when he comes in frae his work or else…

Ma rushes aboot the hoose like she's in a race. She says it's a race against time, no enough minutes in the day. She cannae get a breath. Ah rush aboot efter her, under her feet, tae she shouts, Billy. Sit.

Oor Betty tells on me if ah squirm too much. Ma, he's kickin the table, or, Ma, he's rockin agin.

Oor Cathy jist slaps me roon the heid wi her cloth.

Ma shifts ma seat in straight an looks intae ma eyes wi hers wide as the Clyde. She runs her hauns up an doon ma arms tae she rubs ma jitters away.

Tam spars wi me when he gets in. Ah jump up an go *Wheee ho jo* like a Kung Fu fighter an we dae Chinese kicks. Tam goes *Wheee ho jo* back, goes fer ma ears, then ma tum, then ma legs an ah dodge intae his belly, punchin as much as ah can, but it disnae even shift. He's as hard as Ma's washboard. He grabs me an swings me high by ma middle, his fingers diggin intae ma bones so's ah cannae help it, ah squeals. Ah can see doon his throat tae his tonsils, an his big black eyes ur jist jiggin, so they ur.

Nothin can get me up here, ah'm King o the Castle.

Da bangs the door an sits on the best seat, at the fire, his legs open wide. Ye can smell the Yards aff him, the oil an the sweat an somewhit else steamin aff. Bad temper, Tam says it is, but it's mare like pish tae me. Da sits hunched up. His chin's at his collar an his eyes sink intae they lumpy bags o cheeks but ah'm no fooled, they big hauns ur aye itchin tae smart the skin on boys.

Da disnae say nothin tae Tam. No a word. He jist grunts at him an spits intae the fire, makes it spit back. Tam looks at him sideways ready tae square up, but Da jist grunts noo Tam's big an strong. Tam wid hit him back noo. He widnae let him cut his face agin.

Ma keeps Da away frae me. She gies me the rollin eye tae say yer gettin too loud, Billy. But he'll no hit Ma noo, no since she hid her first heart attack an Tam pushed him against the wall at the hospital, his arm under Da's chin. Da's face wis red as blood an his tongue poked oot tae the doctors came an pulled Tam aff. Noo, even if lumberin aboot on the drink, Da jist curses an grunts at Ma. But he's mean wi the pay packet an she his tae take in washin. She says it's fer extras, like tae pay fer Ginger an oor school stuff.

Ma learns me ma numbers efter the kitchen's cleared cause she says ah'm behind. We sit at the table oot o Da's road. Ma smooths ma hair behind ma ear wi her carbolic fingers, promises me a Jammie Dodger if ah get wan right. Gies me wan even if ah dinnae.

Teacher keeps eyein me an noddin. Keep at it Billy, you can do it Billy. It's sums, sums, an mare sums. Ah'm tryin tae add up but they never add up right. The clock's tickin ower the class door. Ah watch it but it disnae move. Never mind whit Ma says, time's a slow thing, so it is, specially fer a boy who hates sums.

She's a marvellous woman, Ma says. That Missus McLean is a saint, Ma says. An so she is wi they big roon eyes an rosy lips. A pitcher, Tam says. Too bad she's married awready or ah'd ask her masel, he says.

That gied me a fright.

Tam can no way ever get married. Maybe ah could stay wi him an his wife, but then there's Betty. An Cathy. An Ma. An Ginger. Maybe we could aw go. Leave Da tae clear his ain decks.

Ah looks up at the clock agin an gets anither fright. Cause there's Tam starin at me through the roon windae in the door, like he's no got a body. His eyes ur aw swolled up. Maybe oor Betty's forgot hersel an fell under a bus. Or maybe it's oor Cathy. Naw, she's too clever fer that. Ma heart kicks when ah think it might be Da fell intae the furnace at work, or splashed intae the Clyde an got stuck under a hull.

But Tam widnae be greetin.

Missus McLean gets up an goes tae the door an shuts it behind her. Everybody gawps, their mouths open like fish. Ah try tae hear but cannae. Their heads ur both in the glass noo, waverin aboot like they're under the water. The door opens an she slips back in, her big pansy eyes aw wet. She floats ower an takes ma arm, swims me tae the door an Tam gets me roon the chest an sails me doon the corridor an aw the way hame.

Tam's been lookin efter us aw summer tae the dark nichts came in and the leaves aw turned, but he's oot the day cause it's Sunday an that's his day roon at the mates.

Da says tae me, come wi me, you. We've a job tae dae.

Ah dinnae want tae go wi him but ah dinnae want a tannin. He's got his bowls bag an we go doon the hill tae Havoc Shore, me runnin behind him, tryin tae keep up. Ah asks him if ah'm tae get a shot? He laughs at me, the way he does that's no really a laugh, mare like a frog croakin. His face's aw white like he's rubbed it in Vim, an his cheeks've fell in, the bones ur like broken matches.

We pass the Nun's school at Braeside. It looks like a jumble o cardboard boxes on the cliff. An then Died Man's Cave, where Tam tellt me William Wallace hid afore he got took tae London fer tae be drawn, hung an chopped up. Ah run ma fingers ower the red grit an shiver. Tam aye pits me on his shoulder so's ah can see intae the cave but it's no really much o a cave, mare a slit. Ah know better hiding places than that. William Wallace should've had me an oor Tam on his side.

We go on doon the path tae where the river passes an the seagulls swoop aboot. There's naebody else alang the water, cause it's wintertime an naebody comes doon here in the winter. It's fair freezin an ah hiv tae pull ma sleeves doon ower ma fingers. Ah looks back up the cliff tae the hooses, wee matchboxes aboot tae tumble ower the edge. The wind tugs like it wants tae pick me up an throw me away.

When we get tae the shore Da opens the bag an pulls oot a squirmin sack. Ah takes a minute tae get that it's the kittens. The six kittens that Ginger hid an Da disnae like cause they get under his feet. Naebody'll huv em but Tam says it's okay, we'll keep em tae he can find hames. Ah need tae wee an ah must be wrigglin as Da says ah'm tae stop it or ah'll be goin in the fuckin river wi the vermin. Ma chest's sore an ah'm shiverin but ah stay still as ah can. He slips an slides his way doon the bank an ontae the shore, swings the sack high ower the waves tae it sploshes intae the water.

Ah watch fer it tae come up. But it disnae.

The wee soft mouths an the wee noses'll be fillin up an the eyes blinkin in the dark. Warm pee soaks intae ma pants. Da turns, his teeth bitin intae his lip, his nose pinched wi the cauld. No his angry face, mare a look like he's gonna greet. His strands o hair get pulled aw roads by the wind's fingers.

We stand like that fer ages, me peeing masel an him getting wee-er an wee-er, wi the gulls makin circles ower his heid an the wind blowin the long grass aw ways. He drops tae his knees an punches the sky.

Ah bolt up the path, past Deid Man's Cave, past the nuns' school an hame tae hide under the stairs in the dark, tae Tam gets in.

L.O. Evans

L.O. Evans writes experimental fiction and poetry that explores the way that readers interact with the words on the page. Like most millennials, he left university with a liberal arts degree and a lack of real-world skills, yet he has somehow parlayed this into a series of jobs writing for education magazines, volunteering with Bristol-based charities, and teaching at state secondary schools. He is currently working on his first novel, tentatively titled *Milkham*, while completing an MA in Creative Writing at Bath Spa University, where he previously won the 2012 Poetry Prize."

Shapeshifting

"It is most fun and most rewarding to make a shape you yourself create rather than following someone else's plans." – Marion Walter, from '*Constructing Polyhedra Without Being Told How To.*'

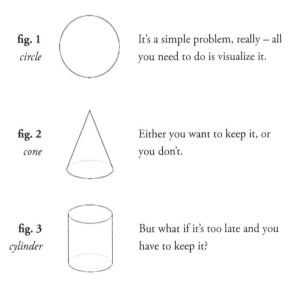

fig. 1
circle

It's a simple problem, really – all you need to do is visualize it.

fig. 2
cone

Either you want to keep it, or you don't.

fig. 3
cylinder

But what if it's too late and you have to keep it?

fig. 4
regular tetrahedron

Or what if you do want to keep it, but you still end up losing it?

fig. 5
square-based pyramid

Will you even be able to live with yourself knowing that, at one point, you didn't want to keep it?

fig. 6
cube

What about if you do want to keep it now, but then you discover later on that you don't want it?

fig. 7
pentagonal prism

Or, worse yet, if it doesn't want you?

fig. 8
regular octahedron

Is it even capable of knowing that you exist yet?

fig. 9
*elongated square
pyramid*

Does it even know that it exists?

fig. 10
*augmented tridiminished
icosahedron*

And how do you plan on telling
them about it?

fig. 11
*augmented hexagonal
prism*

Will they be angry with you if
you choose to keep it?

fig. 12
regular dodecahedron

Will they still look after you if
you don't?

fig. 13
*gyroelongated square
pyramid*

Can you afford for this to
happen?

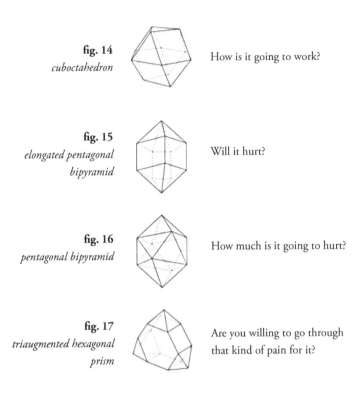

fig. 14
cuboctahedron

How is it going to work?

fig. 15
*elongated pentagonal
bipyramid*

Will it hurt?

fig. 16
pentagonal bipyramid

How much is it going to hurt?

fig. 17
*triaugmented hexagonal
prism*

Are you willing to go through
that kind of pain for it?

fig. 18
quadaugmented cube

Are you willing to make sacrifices for it?

fig. 19
heptadecagonal prism

Are you willing to let it take things from you that you'll never get back?

fig. 20
regular icosahedron

And if not, will there be a chance to have another one?

pl. 1
sphere

Or is this it? *(see fig. 1)*

Jess Farr-Cox

Jess Farr-Cox is a self-employed editor and indexer at thefilthycomma.co.uk; blogs at thefilthycomma.wordpress.com; works overseas regularly as a teacher and educational consultant; and teaches in the Dept. English, University of Bristol. In her copious free time, Jess has been working on a gently experimental (but quietly brilliant) novel for about twenty years, which she hopes to unleash on the world the minute she can persuade the house to clean itself. She also has plans for a short story collection in which each story contains a daffodil.

Dogging

It started out as a joke. His parents had a bloodhound when he was growing up and he kept saying how much he liked big dogs. "Not something yappy," he said, when we passed an old lady walking half a dozen balls of fluff in the park, all of them in matching coats, shiny and striped like biscuit tins. We talked idly about names for a dog, much as other couples might have turned to each other in the evening and said "James. What about James, for a boy? After your father?" He liked the sort of name you might give to a person – Frank, Freddy, Bruno. I liked the idea of naming a dog after something else, like a tree or a plant – Rowan, for example, or Basil. I thought the longing for a dog was a station that we might linger at on the way to a longing for children, hens, an allotment and a shed, and then we moved out of the city and bought a small house with a big garden and that seemed to be as far as we were going to get.

I had thought that we both imagined the fantasy dog as large, slobbery, over-affectionate, stupid and unashamedly male, but, above all, a fantasy. We were wholly unprepared for a real dog – the house was too small, the stairs too narrow, the paintwork too white. The day that I got home and found him playing in the garden with a puppy – a vast puppy that cantered about on stiff legs like a giraffe – was something that surprised me so totally that I stalled the car and drifted silently down the sloping drive. She was a Great Dane, with a black muzzle and pink ears and brown eyes. The rest of her gangly body was a deep, velvety white. She had a tatty piece of rope in her jaws and her paws braced in front of her in a position that I recognized from the yoga classes I now had to drive to every week. He held the other end and they were engaged in what looked like a highly enjoyable tug of war. He was panting and laughing, she was whipping the hedge into a frenzy with her tail.

"Hello," he said, dropping the rope so that she tumbled backwards onto her haunches. "I wanted to surprise you." For all our discussion of names, we called her Narcissa, after a relative of his that he hadn't cared for.

"She even looks like Great-Aunt Narcissa," he had said, regarding her with his head on one side. I found this difficult to believe. He had a tag made with her name on it and bought her one of those enormous leather collars. "Almost big enough for you," he said to me when he got back from the shop, putting it around my neck for a second before he put it on the dog. We also bought a sign to go on the gate that said 'BEWARE OF THE DOG'. We argued in the pet shop about whether we should get one that said 'CAVE CANEM' and was it fair to assume that postmen and assorted delivery people would know what that meant. I said it was a well-known phrase (well-known enough to be written on a £12.99 sign for sale in a pet shop the size of our entire ground floor), and he said it was arrogant to use Latin when we didn't need to and I said what about church, and he said I was changing the subject and we bought 'BEWARE OF THE DOG'. We bought little child gates to go across the stairs, which took an hour to attach to the banisters, and which she immediately stepped over, delicately, lifting her feet up like a cat, looking up with ears raised like eyebrows to see if she had pleased us and then wagging her tail and panting into our faces when she got to the top of the stairs to show she had done something clever.

I decided in a lucid moment that I would chart the stages I passed through, from being abandoned at one end of the process, to becoming myself again at the other. I read a book that talked about Denial and Acceptance and all the stages in between, and so I wrote the words out neatly on a little chart and stuck it on the fridge and put one of her fridge magnets on the chart next to 'Rage' (a blue letter 'm') to show how I thought I was doing.

I could have annotated my chart with my own list of sub-stages: Begging To Be Taken Back; Nasty, Defiant Sex With Ex-Girlfriends; Managing Really Quite Well, Especially When Other People Are Around. Look, I Have Even Cleaned The Kitchen; Unexpected Crumbling In Boots On Realising I No Longer Have Any Need To Purchase Fancy Condoms; Making Mutual Friends Uncomfortable; More Unexpected Crumbling When It Turns Out She Has Met Someone; and so on. None of these seemed to offer me much of a way out. I just cycled round and round, like somebody trapped in a multi-storey car park, going up or down ramp after ramp but never finding the exit. Some days I made progress: taking her unwanted clothes to a charity shop, or conquering a small domestic task that she had always done. Other days I blundered further into the bowels of the car park, onto dark, half-empty floors below street level where nobody but drug dealers and government agents would choose to park, or the upper levels where there was more light, and the opportunity to hurl oneself to a quick death. The magnet wasn't strong enough and my little blue 'm' kept sliding reproachfully down the chart until I flung it into the bin and chose a letter that didn't mock me. And then (on the same day that I broke down in the post office because they started playing 'The Heart of the Matter' on the radio), I moved into the final stage: Driving Around.

I had resolved to clear her clutter out of the car — the bossy satnav, the tins of boiled sweets, the rattling small change, the massive stained road atlas, the emergency blanket that she thought was so important (she never said what the emergency might be. "Just in case," she said. In case of what?). On any given day, I could leave my disinfected home and go to my car and without even trying I could find something she had touched. I could even find something she had put in her mouth, from her habit of starting boiled sweets and then putting them back in their wrapping, blurred and glassy. She was only half gone. I pictured her half-drowned, with chilly shells covering her breasts, and the past as an enormous fish with its jaws straining around her hips, and she looked so cold and cross that I couldn't help smiling. The car needed to be reclaimed from the sea.

I remembered learning about coastal erosion at school, and the more I thought of her as a white-flecked tide that I was going to repel by sitting in the driver's seat (I was Canute, pushing back the waves without even troubling to get up), the more half-remembered terms started to come back to me. Longshore, which sounded like the name of a conquering Viking king (I ignored the softer, vaguer 'drift'. I wasn't interested in drifting). Gabions were definitely involved in some way, and not at all the small items of furniture that they sounded like (I could almost hear her saying 'I don't know where you left it. Are you sure it isn't on the gabion?'). And groynes. The crotchy word, with its extra letters and unfamiliar in the plural, stuck in my mind so thoroughly that I found myself writing it in thoughtful capitals on a Post-it note and sticking it on the fridge next to my chart. I washed her things out of the car in a single movement, like whipping a tablecloth away without disturbing the crockery. I threw out the dangly cardboard pine-tree and the bleached Ramblers' Association sticker and the dead maps and directions to long-forgotten weddings that had burst out of the glove box every time we opened it. I vacuumed the seats and the footwells, and I fancied I could hear grains of sand and tiny shells whizzing into the belly of the machine. I moved through the gears in order rather than block changing as she used to do. I braked smoothly. I indicated in plenty of time. I used my mirrors conscientiously. I always knew what was happening behind my back.

At first I just drove routes that I already knew, right on the speed limit, *changing gears and lanes with aggression and purpose, radio snapped off. I noticed things about the car that seemed new to me, like the smell of the air conditioning and the annoying, iambic indicators. When I reached my destination I didn't pause, just turned around (sometimes a three-point turn in the road as if I was lost) and drove straight home again. In due course, I moved onto something far more entertaining. I would drive to the end of the road, and follow the first car that passed me. Occasionally this backfired, such as when the little white Stylo I pulled out behind turned out to belong to one of my neighbours (she drove around the block and parked outside her house, fifty yards from mine). Subsequent trips were much more successful: a lorry that I followed all the way to the motorway and down to the next junction before night fell; a middle-aged couple in an orange boxy car who were fighting furiously, their heads snapping back and forth, her trying to drive and yell at the same time with her hair swinging out like a skirt as she turned back to look at the road, him leaning over to flip her indicators on and off; a pizza delivery girl on a moped who delivered six steaming boxes to a throbbing house party and never came out again.*

I preferred to drive at night, when the red and white lights left tracers across my vision. When I saw items huddled at the roadside (flowers, sweatshirts, unmated shoes), I stopped and looked at them, or put them in the boot. When I saw a badger curled into itself or partially inside out (these seemed to be the only options), I stopped and lifted it onto the verge with a spade I kept in the car specially. I saw slim, match-footed foxes in the suburbs and ghostly owls on the motorway, and magpies and crows picking at each other's remains. I saw tramps rootling through bins and late night shopkeepers pulling down the shutters, and once a group of students in evening dress walking home. Once it rained and I drove without windscreen wipers. The streetlights gave each raindrop a little golden edge and the red lights of the cars in front were like starbursts, bloodstains and flowers, and that pleased me. Once I drove the same section of road eight times in a row, turning at either end at the mini-roundabouts by going round and round and round until another car (I should say another driver) shamed me into moving on. Once I followed a red Astra to the edge of the moor and watched a couple climb into the back and remove their more constraining outer garments. This, I felt, was the kind of thing I ought to embrace as a single man. I even thought about getting the emergency blanket out of the boot so that I didn't get cold from sitting still (I was amused to see that my horny friends in the Astra had a blanket of similar weight and pattern), when I saw them looking over at me and my idling engine and gesturing to each other. In my rear-view mirror, I could see that another car was lurching slowly onto the track where we had stopped, rattling the cattle grid as it approached. The girl tucked her hair behind her ears in a way that I suddenly understood, and I banged my knuckles on the dashboard as I put the car into gear and drove away in such a way as to convey that the whole thing was a misunderstanding.

She started by chewing my badminton trainers. That didn't matter much, since I had stopped playing when we moved out of the city. I reasoned that she could work out her shoe-chewing issues on that pair and that, by the time they were completely destroyed, she would be through that stage in her development and the rest of the footwear would go unmolested. My trainers kept her quiet for precisely two days (at the end of which she dug up the new vegetable patch and buried one of them in it, laces trailing across the soil like entrails). Then she moved on to my Wellingtons (old, but which I had been about to get a lot of use out of on the allotment); my red heels; and a pair of those Velcro sandals men wear in the summers now. These got him interested in the problem, finally. He rumpled her ears where she sat in the sitting room, surrounded by the wreckage of his shoes. "You must be more careful to leave them out of her reach. She doesn't know any better." Narcissa laid her enormous head in his lap and drooled gently.

"They're your shoes. I didn't leave them anywhere," I said. "And she doesn't know any better because you never tell her off."

"I do. I'll tell her off right now." He pointed at the shredded shoes. "Narcissa?" She looked up at him trustingly, her enormous eyebrows lifted like a plush curtain. "Bad dog!" She pulled a puzzled, wrinkly face that might have been contrite. "See?" he said, turning towards me. "She's sorry." Narcissa celebrated her triumph, not by parading through the streets with chariots and Nubian slaves, but by lying under the dining table while we ate, leaking gas each time I raised the fork to my mouth. "I can't smell anything," he kept saying. "Perhaps it's a poltergeist."

"Ghosts are frightened of cats," I said. "Maybe we should get a cat."

For her next trick, Narcissa got into the bathroom cupboard and ate several tubes of toothpaste. He said I must have forgotten to buy spare tubes when he couldn't find any, but the whitish diarrhoea that she sprayed liberally around the garden suggested otherwise. Then she started pulling packets of food off the worktops or out of the lower cupboards onto the floor and disembowelling them. She could not possibly have considered which foodstuffs would be the most trouble to remove from the kitchen floor, and yet from all the things in the cupboard she would choose a packet of icing sugar or a bottle of absinthe. Having smashed her victim open, she would then proceed to eat a token quantity. This gave her the squits and resulted in more multicoloured turds and/or vomiting. The first time, we found her sprawled across the kitchen floor like an ice-hockey goalie, cuts all over her muzzle and various species of jam pooled on the floor in a sticky Venn diagram. He took her to the vet and picked glass out of her feet and scraped the mess off the tiles. He told her off. Then the next day it was two more jars of jam and a packet of flour that left the kitchen awash with pink goo, and another trip to the vet and more glass on the floor. He told her off again. The vet sent us a bill for two hundred pounds. As he opened it. Narcissa yawned hugely, the roof of her mouth a pink cathedral, her tongue unrolling, impossibly long, as if, bee-like, she had yet more of it coiled inside her head. He paid it without a murmur.

She left me because I didn't meet her needs as a lover. Those were her words. When I asked her what her needs were, she burst into tears. She said she was going to move to Dorset and live in a village I had never heard of and take up pottery. She said there was nobody else involved, but when I said I didn't believe her she shrugged brokenly. Three weeks after she left me, I found out that she had moved in with a man who earns a living by playing the trombone. I don't know if that's relevant.

We walked her most days, and every weekend we put her in the car and drove out for a long walk in the woods. Neither of us were strong enough to hold her on a lead and she seemed to resent any attempt at strapping her down, so we let her canter about. Sometimes she would disappear completely into the trees, but we could still hear her bark booming back to us. He had encouraged her to jump up and put her paws on his shoulders when she was a puppy, to show people how big she was. Now we struggled to explain to her that, muddy and vast, she should no longer expect praise for doing this. She terrorized other walkers, who braced themselves against trees while Narcissa gave their dog's genitals a thorough sniff. "She's very gentle really," I would say apologetically as they rushed off with their violated pets.

He was terribly proud of her, happy to pause again and again and explain her finer points to interested passers-by. "She's a pedigree Great Dane," he would say, reeling off her show name and then pointing out the tiny nick in her ear that made it impossible to show her. "No, I didn't know they came in white either." He even took her on a trip to visit his mother, but she knocked his mother's cleaner down and had to be brought home in disgrace. "I can't understand it," he said to me when they got home. Narcissa was sleeping in her gargantuan bed, a pile of bones. "She's very gentle, really."

He fell over her going down the stairs early one morning. I said he must have seen her – she glows white even in complete darkness – and he said no, he didn't expect to see her on the stairs, she knows she's not allowed on the stairs. He was sprawled in the hall, trying to get up while Narcissa licked him furiously, thrilled to have his face at tongue level. His ankle was badly twisted and I stepped over them both to fetch him some ice. It took me a while to find what I wanted.

"You were a long time," he said, when I returned with a bag of peas.

"She got into the freezer last night," I said. She was still licking him, whining happily and completely convinced that the whole lying down idea was a jolly game for her benefit. Then she spotted me, and leapt up, putting her paws on my shoulders as he had taught her. She was a full head taller than me and her breath stank. I pushed her away. He struggled up and pushed open the kitchen door.

The kitchen was dominated by Narcissa's latest installation (Untitled), and otherwise barely recognisable as a room at all. She had started off by opening the freezer, pulling all the food out of it and piling it into a foodstuff Tower of Babel; then she had changed her mind and rolled around vigorously in the oven chips and defrosting blackberries; then she had eaten several packets of fish fingers and been lavishly sick. She had also, as an afterthought, pulled the blanket out of her bed and trailed it through the vomit. Narcissa broke the silence by lifting her useless lead off the kitchen table and settling down to chew it.

"Narcissa," I said. She did not look up. "Bad dog."

One day, I turned out of the end of the road and picked up a little green car. The entire back seat was filled with the most enormous white dog. It was so big that I wondered if it were real, or if, like a pantomime horse, it might be two men in a costume. They drove over the bridge and into the woods. I pulled in behind them as they got out of the car, the dog bounding around joyfully. She was a milky, mystical animal, like a white hart. As I watched, one of her gorgeous ears flipped itself inside out, a pink beret worn at a rakish angle. The three of them stamped off into the trees, the woman wearing a little woolly hat, the man (live-in boyfriend rather than husband, obvious even from a distance) limping along in impractical shoes and jeans that he had paid someone to distress on his behalf (presumably by telling them that they didn't meet his needs as a pair of trousers).

The road was narrow and turning the car around took longer than it should have. The shortness of the trip annoyed me; there was still so much of the day to fill. Then I saw them coming back, the chap's limp more pronounced, as if he had been in a fight, the woman with no expression at all. The dog was nowhere to be seen. They got back into the car, and in a moment it was gone. Horrible possibilities crowded around me and I was out the door and into the woods in my driving shoes – penny loafers that she bought me when I passed my test at the first attempt, thirty-five years old – through the puddles and the mud. Her barks echoed through the trees, and I found her with her lead tied to a branch, trying to jump, convinced that they had left her behind by mistake and that if she just barked loudly enough they would come back. Her muzzle was black and soft, wrinkled like a prune. I crouched down like I had seen Barbara Woodhouse do on television. She paid no attention at all, barking and barking, drool hanging from her mouth in foaming strands. "Good girl," I said. She looked as if she could take my hand off at the wrist, but I put it out to her, and she allowed me to fondle her ears. They refused to lie flat and although she stopped barking, she kept turning her head and her ears this way and that, listening for the little green car.

Her collar was leather, with a bright silver tag bearing what I eventually realised must be her name. "I won't be calling you that," I said, and I untangled her from the tree.

Sometimes I see her lift her ears, rather as my father used to raise his hat to old ladies, if she hears something with a similar engine note to the little green car. But she sleeps on the end of my bed and answers to her new name and I think that in time she won't remember what happened. She has her own fridge magnet on my chart (a green letter 'e') that covers the last letters of 'Acceptance'. We're going to drive out to the coast next week. I can already picture her romping about in the waves like Moby Dick, holding her face away from the spray and digging enthusiastically for nothing at all.

She likes to stay on the lead when I take her for walks, but sometimes she forgets herself and I let her rush off into the bushes after an intriguing smell. She can be gone for several minutes, leaving me on the path to wait proudly. Occasionally other walkers look at me as I stand still and alone in the mud for no apparent reason, grinning happily. I don't mind. "Evening!" I say brightly. "I'm just walking the dog."

Stacey Gowland

Stacey Gowland is a full time student who lives in County Durham with her husband and two children. She started studying English with Creative Writing at Teesside University in 2014 and is currently working towards a MA in Creative Writing. She spends much of her time reading, immersing herself in other people's stories that transport her to exciting new places and writing stories that will hopefully transport others. She enjoys experimenting with different narrative styles and bringing a sense of realism from her own perspective to her writing.

The Making of Nancy

She walks into the bar and orders a whisky. The counter is sticky with spillages, crusted with the crumbs of nut shells. Brown and flaked. The barman eyes her for a second, his deep-set beady eyes shadowed beneath the bush of unruly brow taking over his forehead. She stares unwavering, daring him to refuse her. She knows she doesn't look old enough to be in here, seventeen and looks younger still. The barman shakes his head, smirking to himself and pours the drink. She knocks it back in one, puts the glass down and orders another. He's disappointed, he wanted a reaction. She pushes the glass toward him nodding, hurry up, get on with it. Resigned, he slops out another shot. Picking up the glass she swivels around on the stool to take in the room. A couple of people sit on tables alone, nursing their drinks, heads bent and hidden in the dingy lighting and dark wood cladding, chipped, and stained. She sparks up a smoke and looks toward two men playing pool in the far corner. The light is brighter there, illuminating the table and its players like actors on a stage. She saunters over, the shake of her hips, the downturn of her eyes, the coy smile, the clip of her heeled boots against the hard floor marking her approach.

Nancy ran out of the store and didn't stop until she reached the park at the end of the block. The boots cradled in her hands. She bent over, clutching her treasure to her chest, and laughed breathlessly. The store assistant's face as he realised she wasn't going to go out with him. His weak attempt to grab her as she turned to run. His face as she imagined it now, outraged, embarrassed, scared. Nancy laughed aloud. She kicked off her trainers, stained from age and wear, and put on the black boots. The buckles shiny and new, the teeth of the zip locking together without resistance. She stuck her feet out in front of her and wiggled them about. The heel would add three inches to her small frame. Nancy stood up and felt invincible.

'You want to play?' The dark haired one asks her.

'I don't know how.'

'Don't worry darlin'. I'll show you how.' He smiles, confident. She agrees to play, missing shots, bending over more than necessary, chalking the cue while glancing toward him. His friend takes the hint and leaves with a wink. She giggles. They play two games, she loses both. She leans into her opponent, her mouth brushing his ear, her breath on his throat, 'Meet me outside in five.' The guy beams and heads outside. She sits back at the bar, orders another whisky, nursing it for ten minutes before going out to the parking lot. He's still waiting. Good. He's leaning against a rusted blue pick-up, the arches ready to crumble. She fingers the gun at her back.

'You remember Sophie?'

He pales.

'So, you do remember her then. Conner?'

He startles up at hearing his name. Inside the bar she had suggested they forgo names insisting it would be fun. He says nothing, his face says everything. She watches the minute changes, the twitch of his lips. The widening then narrowing of his eyes. The drip of sweat that slides down his face, even as the breeze blows cool from the sea, bringing with it tang and salt. She can feel it cling to her skin. A foreign layer of flesh. She pulls the gun from her back and points it at him, cocking it.

He tries to speak, stuttering a noise. It comes out high pitched. She laughs. He looks embarrassed, vanity and pride at the forefront even at a time like this. He looks down scraping his foot in the gravel.

The precarious walk to the lake that night, the ever-moving gravel, the pungent tang of sewage from the nearby plant. None of these deterred teenagers from choosing the lake as the number one hangout for drinking and partying. The boys were daring each other to jump off the train bridge, they had been for an hour, laughing, drinking, getting louder with each swig. Nancy walked to the edge of the water and picked up a stone. Obsidian, oval and smooth. She stroked her fingers along it enjoying the feel, then pulled her arm back and skimmed it across the water. One, two, three jumps, before it disappeared, ripples left behind in its wake. The air balmy from summer, even at this time of night. A breeze blew across the water, her bare shoulders broke out in goosebumps sending a judder through her.

Conner shook. She could see him struggle to control it. To regain his swagger.

'I… I don't know what you want from me?'

'I want you to say her name.'

'Why? What's the point? She was lying. I didn't do nothing. The police cleared me. Stupid bitch made the whole thing up. Begging for it she was, only got scared because she thought her dad might find out and start a shit storm."

'Don't suppose you getting off had anything to do with your uncle being the sheriff?'

Nancy walked into her uncle Stan's store. A dinky convenience that upped the prices so much that it wasn't convenient for anyone. The stockroom door was open a peak, Nancy glanced through the gap. Mary, a girl from Nancy's math class, stood stock still. Her arms limp at her sides. Stan's fat stomach pressed against her, his sausage fingers hooked and absent beneath her skirt. Sweat gleamed his forehead, his few strands of greasy hair plastered against it. His ruddy jowls vibrating. Mary looked at Nancy, pleading. The scene didn't shock Nancy, she wasn't scared. It just was. She hated Stan though, she wanted to hurt him. Nancy walked back to the front of the store, taking her time to pick the most expensive bottle of wine on the shelf. That, she knew would infuriate him more than what she was planning. She strolled back to the stockroom and raised the bottle above her head and brought it down over the back of Stan's skull and rolls of neck. The bottle exploded. Stan's obese frame thudded to the floor. Red wine splashed every surface.

The girls giggled as they listened to the boys, each more boisterous than the one before him, arguing over who should jump first. Nancy was bored.

Tommo swung his arms out to his sides.

'I'm gonna do it! I'm gonna jump!' He stood on the edge, his toes gripping. Nancy left the girls at the lakeside and made her way to the bridge, interested for the first time. Fifteen minutes later, Tommo still hadn't moved. Nancy kicked her shoes off, took a breath and ran past the boys crowding the edge, and jumped. She spread her arms out feeling the wind go through her, nothing holding on to her, nothing to hold on to. Freedom. She hit the water fully clothed, submerged in darkness before springing back up to the surface. The impact echoed through the trees. The disturbed water covering the surrounding stones, trunks, and girls. An owl hooted, annoyed, and flew out of the tree he was perched in.

The road was empty. A lone owl hooted nearby, leaves rustled. Animals scurried through the dense undergrowth and brush of the surrounding woods. Going home, hunting for food. Most of them asleep. The town at the bottom of the hill, usually dark and quiet at this time of night, was a flurry of activity. Sirens wailed, people shouted, voices echoing up the hill unformed, the inclination but not the words. The town glowed. Flames shot forty feet into the air, illuminating the night, the darkness disguised. The flames popped and crackled, debris raining down like fireworks. Nancy smiled at the place she was leaving behind, happy to be going. She wouldn't miss a single thing from that backwards shithole. Not a single person. She left her suitcase at the edge of the rocky bank that lined the road. Separating it from the trees, an unnatural path cut out of nature, giving way to an abomination of nature. She walked to the middle of the road and looked up. The moon was full and bright. Clouds rolled in, threatening. Nancy checked her watch. 2am. She walked back to her suitcase, picked it up and started walking toward her future.

She looks up at the rolling clouds then back to Conner.

'Get in the truck, we're going for a ride.' Conner stares, unmoving. She waves the gun, 'Now!'

Conner stumbles as he opens the door. She climbs into the passenger seat, pulls her seatbelt across her and twists so that she leans on the window and faces Conner.

'Head toward the quarry.' Conner's hands shake as he starts the engine. The truck stutters but rumbles to life. Loud, old, and wheezing. The gears grind as Conner steers out of the carpark. She watches the flickering garish red glow of Bill's Bar in the wingmirror until they round the corner at the end of the road. Conner grips the wheel, blood draining from his hands leaving them ghostly white in the dark. He chances a glance at her, opens his mouth, closes it again. She smirks. His fear sustains her. His fear, all their fear, makes her heart pound, helps her blood to flow. It keeps her alive. Makes her strong.

Nancy was kept back at school. Made to write lines with the other undesirables while Mr Robson leant too close over them. Once home, she opened the fridge to find it empty apart from a half-drunk bottle of schnapps and a pack of beer. She dumped her bag on the bench and trudged to the front room where her mam was sitting, still in the clothes she slept in. The radio blasting in the corner, the windows closed, the curtains drawn. Nancy held her nose against the stench, foist, dirt, stale beer, and smoke. The smell intensified by the lack of air in the room and the sweltering heat. Nancy walked to the window, threw the curtains open and cracked the window. Her mam shielded her eyes against the bright onslaught.

'It stinks in here.'

'I don't smell nothing.'

'That's because the smell is you.'

'Don't think you can come in my house and start talking to me like that.'

'There's no food in again.'

'Ugh, check the cupboards.'

Nancy gave up and walked to her room, sat on her bed, and stared at her reflection in the mirror opposite. Her hair was long. Cornflour blond, with natural white and honey highlights. It hung shiny and straight to rest at her waist.

Conner pulls up to the quarry.

'Get out and start walking.' He makes to take the keys out of the ignition, but she stops him with a shake of her head. She keeps the car idling and the lights on. She looks in the mirror, then walks Conner over to the edge.

The hole is cavernous. Sandstone boulders balancing precariously on cut out shelves that had been made for further exploration. The view beyond goes on for miles undisturbed. Pure flat darkness, with faint lighter and darker patches to mark hills in the land, trees, and brush. The sky above stays clear and bright, the moon full, flanked by blinking stars.

Everyone worshipped her that night. They called her 'jumper' they called her crazy, but they made the names sound like titles. Nancy liked that. Tommo walked over to her, his teeth bright in the full moon, and sat down beside her.

'You trying to show me up back there?'

Nancy shrugged, 'I was bored of waiting.'

Tommo passed Nancy a drink and moved closer. She took a swig and leant back, her eyes closed.

'You want to go for a walk?'

'Maybe in a little while. I'm just listening.'

'To what?'

'Everything.'

Tommo said nothing. Nancy heard a lighter flicker and then the sweet and pungent smell hit her. She opened her eyes and smiled at Tommo.

'You want some?'

'Mmhm.'

Tommo handed it to Nancy. It was badly made. The papers not quite sticking together. The ratio of ingredients disproportionate. Fat and tight in the middle, loose and full of air at the end. Nancy took a draw and held it. It wasn't as good as the stuff she had skimmed off her dad, but it gave her the head change that she needed.

'About that walk?'

'Sure.'

Nancy stood up, her clothes still wet clung to her. Tommo took her hand and led her away from the group, further into the woods. They stopped five minutes in and Tommo leant forward giving Nancy her first kiss. It was awkward at first. Wet, noisy, tongues uncoordinated, but soon they found their rhythm. Tommo's hands reached under Nancy's top, she pulled away.

'Don't go getting all frigid.' He reached toward her again. Nancy hit him hard around his face, her nails scratching him.

'Bitch!' Tommo stomped back toward the lake. Nancy hung back a minute then headed back too. She heard the laughter and shouting before she got there. Tommo's voice carried.

'Well up for it. Yeah. Practically begged me for it.'

The boys laughed, girls giggled and threw the 'slut' word about. Nancy turned around and walked home.

Nancy got up from her bed, walked to the bathroom and riffled through the drawers below the sink until she found what she was looking for. She pulled her hair forward, clutching first one chunk then the other and chopped her hair off at her chin. The scissors chomped down easily. Her hair floated to the ground. She watched it as it glittered and fell like fairies dancing in the sun. It tapped onto the tile floor like spiders walking across a tin roof. She grabbed another chunk at the front and cut in thick bangs that hung low over her eyebrows skimming her lashes. When she was done, she left the scissors on the sink, the hair on the floor, and walked back to where her mam sat on the sofa.

'What have you done!'

Nancy smirked.

'Your dad won't be happy about this.'

Nancy shrugged her shoulders and walked out.

'When I first left home, I was completely alone," She tells Conner. 'It was easier than I thought it would be, but I was still alone. I had to make money, find places to stay, eat. I hitchhiked a lot, met a lot of weirdos. About four months after I first left, I met Sophie. She gave me a ride. She bought me lunch along the way. Then she invited me to stay with her. I stayed with her for three weeks, and in that time, she never asked me for anything. She didn't take her shit out on me. She never lied to me. She never mistreated me. She was good. When I left, she made me promise to stay in touch. Told me I could always come back and stay with her if I needed to. I rang her last month. Do you know what she told me Conner?'

'It's not true! I didn't do anything! She's lying!'

'Get on your knees.'

'What!?'

Mary fell to the floor, then jumped up and ran. Nancy closed the stockroom door, grabbed a chocolate bar, and left. She wandered about town for a few hours, postponing her return home, until it could no longer be avoided. Her dad was waiting on the front steps when she arrived, a beer in his hand. She walked calmly toward him. He stood when she reached the first step. He pulled his free hand to his chest then thrust it out across Nancy's face. She staggered back. Her cheek blazed, her ear rang, her head pounded. Nancy's dad grabbed her hand and dragged her into the house. He shouted for Sandy who came bounding at hearing her name. He grabbed Sandy by the collar and dragged her outside. Nancy ran after them. Her dad attached Sandy to the chain on the fence, then grabbed his shovel. Nancy screamed and tried to grab it away from him. He pushed her back hard, she fell cracking her head. She scrambled to her feet as the shovel made its first impact. Sandy whined then slumped down, her eyes rolling, tongue lolling to one side. Her dad brought it down again, this time with a crack. Nancy lay on the floor staring into Sandy's eyes. Her dad brought the shovel down again, then threw it.

'Stan rang. Don't ever interfere in his business again.' He walked back into the house. Nancy stayed on the hard mud staring at Sandy until the blood reached her. Then she got up and went to the shed.

Nancy waited till her parents were asleep before she climbed out of bed. Her dad had been out drinking with Stan so should be passed out for a good twelve hours. She stashed her suitcase in the shed, grabbed her bike, and headed for town. She checked over her shoulder as she stood outside of Stan's shop, the keys she had stolen from her dad tinkling together. She let herself in and flicked on the torch aiming it around the store, then walked to the counter and helped herself to several boxes of cigarettes. Nancy grabbed four bottles of whisky from the top shelf and put them into the basket on her bike, grabbed another two and poured them around the store. She knocked over the papers and poured another bottle over them then took a lighter from her back pocket, also her dads, and lit the flame. The papers took light quickly. She watched for a second then left the shop and made her way to the school.

Outside the school, she took the lids off the whisky bottles and stuffed them with hankies. Then lit them and threw them through the windows of the science labs. She kept looking over her shoulder as she peddled home to see the flames climbing high and lighting the night sky.

Back home, she used a pocket knife to slash the tires of her dad's car, then grabbed her suitcase and started walking out of town. She could hear the exclamations of people waking to see their town ablaze. Feel the pounding footsteps as people rallied to put out the flames and stop the spread. See the flashing lights of the town's only fire engine. She smiled.

'Why are you smiling?' Conner whimpers.

'Just thinking about another life.'

'Please don't do this. I'm sorry ok? I made a mistake. I didn't mean it.'

'You still haven't said her name.'

She takes a slow deliberate breath and crouches in front of Conner, her breath on his face. She turns to look out over the quarry and watches as the sun starts its slow climb in the distance, then turns back to Conner.

'Sophie.'

'Why do you care?'

'Because people like you need to be punished but never are. Because you think you're invincible, but you're not. Because you think you're entitled to do what you want, but you can't.' She stands and aims the gun.

'Ok! Ok! Sophie! There, I said it. Is that it? Sophie! Sophie! Sophie!'

She pulls the trigger. The resounding boom echoes through the quarry. The bullet goes straight through, taking blood and brain with it. Conner slumps to the floor. She stays to watch the sunrise, then climbs into Conner's truck and drives off to wherever the gas will take her.

Pamela Hensley

Pamela Hensley lives in Montreal. Her short stories can be found in literary journals in Canada including *The Dalhousie Review* and *EVENT* magazine. She was longlisted for the *Humber Literary Review's* Emerging Writers Fiction Contest and was a finalist for the *Malahat Review's* Far Horizons Award for Short Fiction. Recently, she started work on her first novel.

What Remains

Piers meets Carsten at a bakery on Luegallee while his wife is still in bed. Crammed together in line, both carrying infants, they feel obliged to nod to one another. One baby is sleeping against her father's chest, the other is gurgling loudly. How old? Piers asks. Four months, Carsten replies. They share a knowing smile and Piers orders four breakfast rolls and half an apple strudel. The next Saturday morning, they see each other again.

Piers, an expat engineer from Canada.

Carsten, a German doctor who prefers southern climes.

Lise joins Katie for coffee at Katie's place, the ground floor flat of a narrow townhouse that has access to a garden. I've signed up for swimming lessons with Rosalie, why don't you come? Katie asks as she pours out two cups. The thermal carafe a wedding gift from Piers' brother in Canada. Swimming lessons at this age? Not lessons, really, just a bit of fun. Ah, so they won't be afraid. They take the children together each Wednesday afternoon to the large swimming hall in Flingern. The U75 to Oberbilker Markt, change at Oberbilker Markt, the 706 to Kettwiger Strasse.

Katie, an expat journalist from Canada.

Lise, a German medical student who speaks fluent Spanish.

Katie walks down Old Woodward Avenue on a cold Tuesday morning to get a coffee at Einstein's Bagels. The town is not typical, Piers tells Katie, it's not really Detroit, it's hardly USA. They are thirty kilometres from the Canadian border, or twenty miles as they say here. She passes a man in a green hip-length jacket who is walking a Weimaraner. The man nods at Katie and she smiles as they pass but they do not know each other. Katie doesn't know anyone in town, not this man, not the next one, not even her neighbours. We should ask the neighbours to dinner, Piers says, and Katie agrees but she never asks them. At Building 1 in Dearborn, Piers designs engines for cars that will go into production in another four years. He is at his desk by 6:30 in the morning and he stays until most of his colleagues have gone home.

Piers' daughter already has a few dark curls but Carsten's daughter is bald, only a little peach fuzz on top. Both heads are sticking out of BabyBjörn carriers. Only four months, you say? March 11. March 27. Ha! That's pretty close. They shuffle forward in line. The bakery on Luegallee is packed on Saturday mornings but the women work hard behind the counter and the line is always moving. Each week the men buy the same thing as before, four breakfast rolls and half an apple strudel for Piers, three croissants and a loaf of Schwarzbrot for Carsten. They like to go out early so their wives can sleep late and wake up to fresh baked goods on the table.

On the U75 from the swimming hall in Flingern, Katie stands in the aisle with Rosalie in the BabyBjörn while Lise takes a seat nearby. What is the probability that Lise will get the same seat next week when they take the tram again? What are the odds that it will be Lise in that seat on any given afternoon? Rosalie kicks her tiny feet, grabs at Katie's wet hair, says Mamamamamama until Katie kisses her face.

An Airbus A320 features a single aisle layout that typically seats 150 passengers but can fit 180 on a high-density, short-haul flight. Its advanced technology includes innovative weight-saving composites that save fuel for airlines while improving the material strength and durability of the aircraft. It boasts a centralized fault-display for easier maintenance, fly-by-wire controls for increased safety, and a fuselage seven inches wider than competitors' for better passenger comfort.

Lise lays a blanket down on the sand while Piers lights the coals under the grill. End of August, end of summer, they decide to spend the day at the beach instead of in the garden.

There's something free and beautiful about water, Katie says, looking out towards the horizon. It goes on forever, Lise says, like the future. I can't see to the other side. I can see the future, Carsten says. We're working in a hospital in Barcelona and our friends are visiting us with news of Germany. Te amaré en España, Lise says. Katie rolls her eyes.

The entrance to Einstein's Bagels is covered by a copper, dome-shaped awning. Katie pulls hard on the door, steps inside, feels warm air rush around her. Minus ten today, or plus fifteen as they say here. A line has formed in front of the counter, a thick velvet rope strung up to make an aisle. There are four customers in front of her, two students whispering and laughing, an old woman in a white, puffy coat, and a man wearing a bright orange safety vest. Katie does not know these customers, she doesn't know anyone in this town. We should ask the neighbours to dinner, Piers says, and Katie agrees but she never asks them. She takes her place behind the man in the safety vest and looks at the baskets of bagels behind the counter.

Katie asks Carsten, How did you find our flat? He shrugs. I took my chances. There are only so many ground floor flats on this block with name plates that are not German. He is standing in the living room with Julia in the BabyBjörn, her bald head sticking out. He has brought four breakfast rolls and half an apple strudel. I hope he's feeling better soon, he says. But it's kind of you to make the effort, Katie says. She nods then stops smiling and rushes out to the kitchen. When she comes back, she hands Carsten a piece of paper with her phone number written on it. Will you give this to your wife? she says and he takes the paper from her, puts it in his pocket.

Piers turns the sausages so the dark grill lines are on top, six spicy, six mild, take your pick. He works from the outside in, waving away the smoke, turning each sausage with care, pressing it down until he hears a sizzle. From where he's standing he can see Katie and Lise talking on the blanket. If he squints, he can make out the others in the water. Carsten is twirling Rosalie like an airplane, he flings her into the waves. Julia shrieks and Carsten reaches over, grabs his daughter by the wrist and the ankle. Is she nervous? Lise asks Katie while rubbing sunscreen on her shoulders. I think I'm more nervous than she is. Don't be. But what if the teacher doesn't like her? Or what if she doesn't do well? Are you kidding? Rosalie? A little white cream remains on Lise's fingertips, she rubs into the back of her hand. That girl will be head of the class.

Every kind of bagel a person could want is on display in a wire basket: plain, poppy seed, sesame seed, onion and cheese, cinnamon raisin, blueberry, 9-grain, potato, pretzel, asiago. Three flavours of cream cheese can be spread upon the bagel: plain, smoked salmon, and onion and chive. The cheeses are also available in reduced-fat versions.

Sun streams in through the sliding glass door that leads out to the garden.

Everyone wants to go, Rosalie is telling her father, but there are only sixteen spots. What if Julia gets to go but I don't? What if I get to go but not Julia? Piers is lying on the couch watching football on TV, Mönchengladbach vs. Bayern Munich. You get to go but not Julia? he says. Papa, you're not listening. Piers turns his head to look at his daughter. Sorry, sweetheart. I hope you both get to go, though I think your mothers will miss you. He stares at the girl until a cheer from the crowd turns his head back to the TV.

The girls come running back from the shore, peeling off their clothes. Papa! Come with us! We're going in! Julia shouts, throwing her t-shirt on the blanket and laughing at Rosalie who has fallen onto the sand. In two more days they will start grade one at the grammar school on Salier Strasse. Katie and Rosalie will walk from their house to Julia's house and the three of them will walk to school together. If Lise is not on shift at the hospital she will pick up the girls at the end of the day, otherwise Katie will do it. Two massive backpacks to carry their books, two cloth lunch bags, eight DIN A4 lined notebooks, four mechanical pencils, four PVC-free erasers, two 15-cm rulers, two 30-cm rulers, two glue sticks, and a Schultüte each, filled with gummy bears, sour worms, balloons, and surprises.

Lise is sitting on a hard, plastic seat on the U75 on a Wednesday afternoon. Carsten wants to move to Barcelona, she tells Katie, who is standing. He told me. But why? I'll never leave Germany. That's because you chose it. But it's different for Carsten, Germany chose him. Julia is sleeping in her mother's arms but Rosalie is laughing and trying to speak. Mamamamamama she says until Katie kisses her face.

Experts agree that flying is far safer than any other method of transportation.

In 2013, the total number of fatalities from airplane accidents in Europe was 8, whereas 1,130 people died in railway accidents and 16,932 from road accidents (data available for 20 out of 28 EU member states). Thanks to improvements in the structural and mechanical parts of planes, and the increased sophistication of navigation systems, the crash rate has been in steady decline since the 1950s. Today, the likelihood of being killed in flight is far less than being struck by lightning.

They are such good swimmers, Carsten leaves the girls at the shore so he can join his wife and friends on the beach. One day they will be lifeguards at the swimming hall in Flingern, he says to Lise, smiling and accepting a towel. End of summer, end of August, they have decided to drive to the beach instead of staying in the garden in the city. Piers hands Carsten a beer after he's dried off and the two men hang back behind the grill. Try a sausage, Lise says over her shoulder. Piers hands him a spicy one and says, Or you can have mild, like the ladies. Carsten shakes his head and smiles again. He eats the spicy sausage.

Katie takes her coffee to a table, sits down and unzips her jacket. She hasn't bought any kind of bagel because she couldn't decide which kind. The old woman in the white, puffy coat is gone and so is the man in the safety vest but the students are sitting two tables over, they have taken out laptops and are setting up to work. I'm glad the girls know how to swim, Lise once said to Katie on a blanket in the sand. I won't worry about them when they're teenagers and want to go to the beach with their friends. Behind them Piers roasted two kinds of sausages, one spicy and one mild, take your pick. Katie removes her jacket and sets her gloves aside, stands up and looks for a paper napkin. Poppy seeds litter the surface of the table, a ring of coffee has left a stain.

The odds of Rosalie going on the school trip to Barcelona are 16 in 40, the same as Julia's. The odds of both girls going are 16 in 104.

When lunch is ready, Katie calls the girls away from the water's edge. Two grilled sausages, two tiny bread rolls, two bunches of grapes, a bottle each of Holunder Bionade. They remain standing while they eat at the blanket's edge, their feet sandy, their hair wet and dripping down their backs. Rosalie says to Julia, Let's get seats that are next to each other. Then she puts the Bionade bottle to her lips, tips it up until red liquid runs out her mouth, down her chin. Lise says, You might not get the choice, Schatz. Your teacher might assign you a seat. Rosalie's mouth falls open, her eyes well up. But I don't want to sit next to anyone else! Don't worry, Julia says, taking Rosalie's hand. I will sit next to you. You will sit where the teacher tells you to sit, Lise says, raising an eyebrow. Julia whispers into Rosalie's ear, the girls lock arms and run back into the water.

The students two tables over from Katie are laughing as they work on their laptops. They eat cinnamon raisin bagels with plain cream cheese spread on top and lick their fingers instead of using a napkin. Katie sips her coffee from a paper cup and reaches for a newspaper someone else has left behind. The Red Wings lost 4-3 in overtime. The Pistons are in a five-game slump. The sun streamed in through the sliding glass door that led out to their garden.

Piers is at his desk by 6:30 in the morning and he stays until most of his colleagues have gone home. Sometimes, in the middle of a morning meeting, he hears a plane fly overhead.

Lise is collecting the girls down the beach, Piers is packing up the grill.

In two days' time, Katie and Rosalie will walk from their house to Julia's house and the three of them will walk to the grammar school together. If Lise is not on shift at the hospital she will pick up the girls at the end of the day, otherwise Katie will do it. Will you still move to Barcelona one day? Katie says to Carsten. They are sitting on the blanket, looking out at the water, watching Lise call out to the girls. He smiles. One day, maybe, or what's the point of learning Spanish? The girls are showing their sand castle to Lise, she is inspecting it from every angle. When I am old and still living in Düsseldorf – Katie says. Carsten says, I will visit you.

Piers joins them on the blanket, the grill packed and set aside, and the three of them wait for the others to come back. They are contemplating the long drive home when Carsten remembers the surprise he brought for the girls: sparklers. He jumps up and looks for the bag where they are packed, asks Piers where he can find the matches. Before they leave, the men hold the sticks at arms' length and let the girls light them.

Oooooh! Rosalie cries.

Aaaaah! Julia cries.

Bursts of bright light, brilliant white, flash against a pale blue sky. Smoke rises up when the flames die down, ashes fall to the ground.

Rosalie says: it's not fair, I don't even want to go if you're not going. Don't be stupid, Julia says, you won the lottery. Besides, we'll go again in the summer. She is upstairs in Rosalie's bedroom sitting on the bed, lying on the bed, sprawling across the floor while Rosalie packs her suitcase. Eight pairs of underpants, two cotton bras, one pairs of jeans, two pairs of shorts, six t-shirts, a bathing suit, a pair of sandals, a nightgown, and a gift for her host family. Every one of the forty students who studies Spanish at the Gymnasium wanted to go to Barcelona. *Hola*, Julia says in a deep voice from the floor, *mi nombre es Rosalía...*Shut up!*...y estoy en busca de* *un amante español*...Rosalie throws a pillow in Julia's direction while Julia rolls onto her stomach.

Katie puts the sports section of the newspaper aside and looks instead at the front page. Arson is suspected in a blaze at a distillery. The price of natural gas is expected to fall. The Auto Show at Cobo Center has attracted more than 800,000 visitors. At Building 1 in Dearborn, Piers is designing engines for cars that will go into production in another four years. The engines will be shipped to assembly plants around the world, he tells his wife over dinner, including the one in Cologne. Maybe I will have to visit Cologne and you could come with me then, Katie. Katie smiles at Piers but they both know she will never go back to Germany. They sailed on the Queen Mary from Southampton to New York and drove from New York to Detroit. She will never make another overseas trip, she will never get on another airplane. One of the students two tables over has long, dark hair, the other is pale and blonde.

For security reasons, since 9/11 all cockpits have been retrofitted with reinforced doors that are intruder-proof and bulletproof. They can now withstand hand grenade blasts. The normal procedure for a crew member to enter the cockpit is to request permission from the pilot through an intercom and for the pilot to open the door. If a crew member does not get a response from the pilot, he or she can enter an emergency code into the keypad and gain access this way instead. Only if the pilot's toggle is set to lock, will the keypad be disabled. In this case, the door will not open for five minutes. A double guard against forcible entry.

It's cold and grey on the morning when Katie wakes up with the knowledge that one day she'll forget. She'll be driving the car and suddenly realize she no longer remembers if it was a Tuesday or a Wednesday that she and Lise used to take the girls to the large swimming hall in Flingern. That it was the U75 to Oberbilker Markt and the 706 to Kettwiger Strasse. That they left from the ground floor flat together. That Rosalie's favourite cake was ginger. That when they lived in Germany, Piers's hair was black not white.

The town is not typical, Piers tells her when they move, it's not really Detroit, it's hardly USA. They are thirty kilometres from the Canadian border, or twenty miles as they say here. Coffee tastes the same in Detroit as it does in Düsseldorf. It tastes the same at 38,000 feet in the air. It wasn't fair that Rosalie got to go on the school trip and Julia didn't. But it's not her fault, Lise said when she stopped in to say goodbye. She won the lottery. The snow is cleared from the streets by the City, but shop owners are supposed to salt the sidewalks. Last year, a woman slipped outside Einstein's Bagels, breaking her hand in the fall. To compensate for loss of wages, and for pain and suffering, she sued the shop owner and the corporation for half a million dollars. Beneath Katie's feet, the salt is hard as crystal pellets. It leaves blurry white rings on the suede of her boots and gets stuck inside her treads.

Thirteen days after her fourteenth birthday, Rosalie is screened with a metal detector and her backpack is sent through an Xray machine before she boards the Airbus A320. The only liquids she is carrying are in containers no larger than 100 mL and they are inside a re-sealable bag. It is a warm, clear day in Barcelona, the wind is blowing at 6 km/hr NNW. The flight attendant accepts Rosalie's boarding pass, points her way to a seat down the aisle on the far side of the cabin.

At 10:28, the plane reaches a cruising altitude of 38,000 feet above the majestic French Alps. The seatbelt light goes off, passenger seats recline, the captain gets up to use the washroom. At 10:30, the cockpit door to the Airbus A320 locks. At 10:34 the captain presses the intercom and requests permission to be let back in. The co-pilot, a younger man who has been treated for depression, makes no attempt to answer.

Katie takes Rosalie's favourite ginger cake out of the oven, annoyed at herself for having left it too late to make the icing. Julia knocks on the door, calls hello, comes into the kitchen, says they have to go. Katie nods and throws the oven mitts onto the counter, checks her hair in the glass of the cupboard door before grabbing her keys off the window ledge.

At 10:41, French authorities lose contact with the aircraft. It's in a steady descent and the captain is begging to be let back into the cockpit. The co-pilot has put the toggle in the lock position, the keypad is disabled. For security reasons, since 9/11 all cockpits have been retrofitted with reinforced doors that are intruder-proof and bulletproof. They can now withstand hand grenade blasts.

There are no survivors in the crash, says the French interior minister. From the black box recorder, investigators conclude the captain was locked out of the cockpit. He is heard banging repeatedly on the door while passengers scream in the background. Because of the terrain, it will take several days to bring down what remains of the bodies. The French president promises that everything will be done to determine the cause of the crash.

Bethan James

Bethan James is a writer from Wales who works for a book PR agency in London. She was a winner in Neil Gaiman & Word Factory's Fables for a Modern World short story competition and her novel *The Lost Magician* was longlisted for The Literary Consultancy's 2017 Pen Factor Prize. Bethan was shortlisted for the inaugural London Book Fair Trailblazer Award which recognises the rising stars under 30 in publishing. Her short stories have been published in magazines such as Litro, and she is a recipient of New Writing South's New Buds Award. Twitter: @thebethanjames.

Waste

They'd strung him up like a runner bean. Straight dangling there. Mom told me to squeeze my eyes real tight like a good girl and not to look, but any idiot knows that makes kids want to peek even more. He wasn't the first one that year.

Mr Jacobs thought no one would spot if he snuck a bit of extra liquid ration. He loved that purple *orkid*, or whatever it was called, like a baby. Growing stuff that couldn't be eaten or crafted was banned. All that flower did was sit there hidden behind his cabin looking pretty. The ORBs see everything though. Wasting water is the worst crime possible. Mr Jacobs was an old man. Mom said he was a waste of water too.

Mom had spoken to me about a time when not everything was desert. When water gushed out from these metal pipe things whenever you wanted it. I was glad I didn't remember. No one misses what they don't know in the first place. But I always did hate feeling the Thirst. That's something you don't ever forget. The way it swallows your belly inwards. Cracks your lips. Yellows your eyes.

One time, Ruth from school told me to walk around with my tongue sticking out of my mouth, like how the wild dogs do on the dunes. She said it would make the Thirst better. So I did, and my tongue ended up swelling like a big piece of dried fruit. Then she started laughing and saying

I can't believe how stupid you are Sam, and waved for Paul to come over so she could tell him what I'd done. Then I threw sand in her eyes. She begged for water to wash it out and grasped at her face. People who waste water are a waste of water, I reminded her, and walked away. She stopped laughing then.

I heard there were kids like us across the other side of the dunes. Except they were taller and wore clean clothes, not mucky jeans. Had bones that didn't look sharp enough to cut yourself on. But maybe it's a lie? No one here ever crosses the sands because of the wild dogs.

When the water tanker rolled into town, all of us wanted to be the first one there. Can't think why. Everyone got the same. A standard bucket ration each. Men and women. Girls and boys. Sick or well. Didn't matter if you were front or back in the queue. Mom said we shouldn't rush out of the porch whenever we heard its engines approaching (not that we had the strength to anyway). It's uncivilised, what would your Daddy think, Sam? Nothing, I said, 'cos he ain't here. I saw water droplets appear in her eyes, but she didn't let them escape, and I felt glad.

A while back, Daddy had been keeping this little white kitten up in the attic, and taking care of it every day. Bringing it food and water. He told me not to go in the attic, so of course I went right up there when he was out at work in the de-sal plant. It looked like one of those snowball things I'd seen in books. I expected it to feel cold. White is a cold colour. But it was clammy and soft and its fur tickled the palm of my hand. The attic dust made it sneeze tiny kitten sneezes. I think Daddy knew I went up there, 'cos I was never quite strong enough to shut the door properly behind me.

One day, Daddy never came home from the plant. People who waste water are a waste of water themselves. My Mom had told me that. My head teacher had told me that. My Daddy had told me that before they strung him up like a runner bean too.

I remember when the ORBs first visited my school. Miss Perkins explained it meant the Organization for Research of Bio-something-or-other. One of them did a presentation to our class. She stood there at the front in a cloud-coloured suit that was untouched by the dust devils outside.

She took questions from pupils at the end. I stuck my hand right up and asked how come her clothes were so clean when there's extra emergency water quotas in place? I thought that made me sound smart. I wanted to impress her. She just tilted her head to one side then smiled, and didn't even bother to answer. My cheeks flushed even more than usual from my stupid question and I kept my hand down by my side from then on.

Most kids asked for more water. The white-suited lady told them it would be soon, in her soft voice. New methods were being researched. We all needed to be patient, pull together and give it more time. Then she started asking us questions, taking each person to the small classroom out back, one by one. But it was the afternoon and I was so thirsty I couldn't think straight and I don't even remember what she asked me. My eyes were all fuzzy and when she spoke I picked at the scabs that ran up my arms like little bugs and never seemed to go away.

Class finished early that day. A reward from the ORBs. We were promised extra nutrient sachets. They must've been pleased by what we'd said somehow. My whole body felt like one big dry mouth, and my brain thumped the backs of my eyeballs. I couldn't wait to get home soon.

When I stepped over the porch, I thought Mom would come and greet me with a hug like usual. She didn't. I guess she wasn't expecting me back so early. Sand had got into the hallway again. I decided to tip-toe across the floorboards. It would be a nice surprise for her. She sometimes sighed and said to me that nothing surprised her anymore.

When I got to the kitchen, I saw my Daddy on top of the table. Well, it looked just like Daddy. A *painting*, I think it's called. Propped up there. But it wasn't quite finished. His eyes were missing. White blanks hovered in the middle. Mom stood with her back to me. She hadn't heard me yet.

Half a glass of clear water rested on the table in front of her. I licked my cracked lips. Mom held a thick paintbrush in her right hand. Then she took that brush and thrust it right into the water. The glass of clean water. She whirled it around until it became a murky tornado.

I couldn't hold it in any longer. I gasped, sucking the room's hot air right between my lips. Mom span around fast. Her eyes were as blank as the portrait's when she looked at me.

She stretched her arm out to grab something. I saw the glint of creeping sunlight on metal. I saw the floor. Such a waste of all that liquid.

Sarah Burton Kennedy

Sarah Burton Kennedy lives in London and works for The Society of Authors where she advises authors on contracts and sells rights for literary estates represented by the SoA. She has a MA in Romantic period literature from the University of Leeds. Her work has been shortlisted for the Ilkley Festival short story competition and she is currently working on a short story collection.

Chestnut Avenue

They began to cut the trees down early in the morning. A safe circumference was established then enforced with high metal barriers and there were security guards and a police presence. People began to gather and they were asked to move back. We're not doing anything wrong, we've a right to stand here, sneaky bastards starting first thing – these were some of the things they said. They watched for a while as one tree after another began to come down and disappear behind the barriers. The chestnuts were at their autumnal best, all rusted leaves and dripping with conkers, and they fell like decorated warriors on a battlefield. The locals shook their heads and someone said it was an outrage, and someone else said what a pity. But their fight had gone after months of protest. They began to drift off. A few with the leisure to do so retreated to the Common cafe and sat at the picnic benches outside and drank hot drinks from thick-rimmed white mugs and inhaled the smell of overused cooking fat coming from inside and shook their heads a little more each time another tree fell. The morning wore on.

There were others at the cafe who knew little about the trees and only wondered at the racket and some complained that it was a strain to make themselves heard above the noise. A couple, who had met online, were on their third date and this one was momentous because it was taking place in daylight and without alcohol. They sat on opposite sides of a picnic bench and drank coffee and she thought how she hated the way he slurped his drink. He wasn't sure she had told the truth about her age. There was a retired man who had sacrificed his late morning pint in the pub to come here and witness this *travesty*, as he had been calling it. A cup of tea and a piece of cake for elevenses, he hadn't done that since his wife had died. There's a bench down there dedicated to my Eva, he said to a woman who sat alone eating a sandwich with one hand and holding an open book in the other. He gestured towards somewhere out of sight, behind the barriers. Oh? I'm sure it won't be damaged, the woman said. That felt like a reassuring to say. He appeared to need reassurance. Presumably Eva had been his wife. She waited before taking another bite of her sandwich in case he expected something more from her. She was on an early lunch break. It was the only time in the entire day when she was responsible for no one but herself. Her plan had been to sit here and read and not speak to anyone. Yet she couldn't help being polite to this old man while also feeling desperate and clutching at the minutes like they were fifty pound notes falling through her fingers and she was down to her last pennies. It won't be the same now though, he said, she wouldn't recognise the place anymore. I suppose not, the woman said. I'm Albert by the way, he said. She finished her sandwich and told him it had been nice to meet him and moved on. She would walk for the rest of her hour. For Eva, who loved this place, read the plaque on the bench for Albert's wife. The trees had been there over a hundred years and all down the avenue running through the Common there were benches beneath their canopy bearing dedications. For Olive and Peter, together always. Cherished memories of Margaret Hull. In memory of Alice Jeffries - people often paused by that one, uncertain at first why but the name rang a bell. It had been all over the news twenty years ago, her face on the front cover of the newspapers.

The search for who did it. The wrong person arrested at first, delaying the search for the right one. Talk of incompetence and enquiries, and compassion for the children, too young to understand and adults by now. What had become of them, with such beginnings. Behind the barriers, the trees were fed into a chipper and ground to mulch.

A waitress came outside holding a plate in each hand. Number twelve, she called out. Number twelve? Anyone number twelve? she shouted. At last someone held up a wooden spoon with the number twelve painted on it. She couldn't understand why people didn't pay attention when they knew they were waiting for food. It was always like this. Standing here like she was in a bingo hall calling out the numbers. Customers ignoring her. At the table she put the plates down and brought her hands to the small of her back where it hurt and asked if they wanted any sauces. They wanted ketchup. She went back inside and returned with a bottle shaped like a tomato that was sticky to the touch. Albert told a mother feeding her baby that it would be thirty years at least before the new trees they were putting in to replace the chestnuts were mature. He imagined how they would begin to grow and flourish as he became correspondingly older and more diminished. It would only be when his grandchildren – if he had any – were grown up that there would be shade once more for picnics and for children to play on a hot day and he would certainly be long gone by then. He wondered again when his son would meet someone and settle down. He had never been introduced to any girlfriends. He was starting to have suspicions but didn't know how to begin to talk about that. Eva would have known what to do. The wind picked up and rippled through other trees across the Common: plane trees, silver birches, oak, sycamore, all those that had escaped the sentence of the chestnuts, and the leaves came off and blew upwards in the air before settling down on the grass for a moment until they were whipped up and rose in the air again in a rough crackle. Some of the locals at the cafe recognised the woman who had organised the protests moving along the barriers and sticking pieces of paper up at regular intervals. She disappeared as she worked her way round the perimeter, followed at a short distance by a security guard. Some moved closer and saw that each piece of paper had the same poem printed on it. The poem was a lament for the trees. In parts, it was angry. The author wasn't named. It was by the woman. The one who had led the protests.

A weekly walking club for the over sixty's gathered outside the cafe. They greeted one another by name and each of them had a pair of sticks like they were planning to go up hills and they wore thick-soled walking boots. The club leader Patrick raised his voice above the chatter and said, I believe we are all present and correct, and they set off in a rustle of unnecessary waterproofs following him towards the north of the Common. Rose pointed out the frame of a bike chained to a post and said to Jean, there are some sharks around. The wheels had been stolen and the saddle. Then Jean and Rose talked again about how poorly they had slept and Jean remarked that it was like when her children were babies, all this going over sleepless nights and finding comfort in another mother's exhaustion. Rose didn't reply, she'd never got to know about all that and she wondered if Jean might ever develop some sensitivity on the subject. She picked up the pace and Jean grew breathless and quiet as she tried to keep up. Freddie and Helga followed close behind them and he was telling her: I'm at my wit's end, no one will help. I don't know how to make her go. She does the most peculiar things for no particular reason. The motion of a falling tree made them all turn and look back and pause as if out of respect for its passing and then they continued onwards and Freddie resumed, I don't want to be cruel, I know she's not well. But I'm living in fear. Helga didn't know what to say. She could have told Freddie it wouldn't end well when he offered to put this friend of his up. I'll never do anything kind again, he said. It makes me sad to hear that, Helga said.

Crows and pigeons clustered around the picnic benches looking for crumbs. They moved towards where the baby in its highchair had thrown food on the floor. He kicked his arms and legs and the mother lifted him out of the highchair and sat him on her lap and he rested his head on her shoulder. There was an eyelash on his cheek and she blew it away and made a wish for him to find a passion in life and to be good enough at it but not brilliant. Let there be no object other than pleasure in the thing itself, whether it's music or sport or drawing or dancing or something else. She didn't look at the old man who kept trying to talk to her. She had enough of that on the bus yesterday. There are too many children in the world, a bearded man with a sour odour had said to her as she did her best to stop her son crying. Her eyes stung with tiredness. The couple on their third date had finished their coffees and he wanted to propose a walk. Coming home last night and finding the silence and stillness in his flat so heavy that he'd started vacuuming at nine pm – he'd had enough of that. He had decided he didn't really mind if she was older than she said. The proprietor of the cafe stood in the doorway wearing a stained white apron. A dog walker had stopped to talk to him. But if they're diseased like they say and a tree fell down and killed someone, wouldn't people ask why nothing had been done. Albert turned to the dog walker and said, you don't seriously believe they were rotten, this is about money. He didn't really know precisely how it was about money, but most things seemed to be, and it was something he had heard at one of the protests. The dog walker and the proprietor ignored him. Albert felt that no one really wanted to hear what he had to say. He had noticed how people often edged away when he started talking and he had the increasing sense of being in the way. You shouldn't have had a say, that's what a lad in the pub had said to him when Albert couldn't help joining in a conversation about Brexit. It won't affect you, the kid said. Younger folk looked forward to getting the likes of him out of the picture, as if he were a burden they resented. He wasn't energetic like the walkers who had done a circuit of the Common and were back at the cafe now for hot drinks and cakes.

Jean remarked that Percy's had been a nice send off on Monday and there were nods and murmurs of agreement. It felt like they were all gathering at funerals every other week, singing hymns if it was that kind of affair, and always queuing up at buffets and piling up paper plates with quiche and sausage rolls and cheese straws. It seemed like someone was gone each time the walking club met. Not surprising really, they were all getting on. Jean had already had to change the numbers for the club's Christmas party booking three times. But you had to book early these days. She eyed Eddie's wide back at another table, stooped over his slab of cake, and thought she would be damned if he came to her funeral before she went to his. The mystery of the club's missing petty cash was not a mystery to Jean. On the south side of the Common a child stood on tiptoes and had to shout to make their order heard through the window of an ice-cream van. Over at the tennis courts, an instructor giving a lesson gazed over the head of his pupil and looked at the empty sky where the chestnut tree tops had been. The couple on a date parted company after she looked at her phone and found something had come up that demanded her immediate attention. A man did press-ups out in the middle of the grass where he could be seen. Joggers completed multiple laps of the Common, overtaking Albert on either side like water flowing around a stone as he drifted off in the direction of the pub, and their breath came heavily and their sweat dripped and their knees took the impact again and again.

Rhiannon Lewis

Rhiannon Lewis was raised on a small farm near Cardigan on the West Wales coast. She studied Welsh, English and Drama at Aberystwyth University and spent five years as a teacher and lecturer. After gaining a master's degree in education, she went on to work in public relations, marketing and communications. She has won prizes for her short stories and in March 2018, her first novel, *My Beautiful Imperial*, was included on the Walter Scott Prize Academy's recommended list of historical novels.

The Significance of Swans

In hindsight, it was the swans that gave 'them' away. Before then, I had never thought of swans as anything other than beautiful birds that graced an occasional river. They would glide by, imperious, mostly indifferent. They seemed oblivious, sleekly unconcerned.

But that day, when we saw seven of them flying over, I turned to my brother and said, 'Geese?'

'No,' he answered. He sounded sure, but there was a hint of bafflement in the voice. 'Swans.'

I stared closer. Yes, swans. 'I don't think I've ever seen one fly,' I said.

'Or calling,' he replied. 'Listen to that noise.'

What was it? A wail? A lullaby? It was both haunting and discordant.

I vaguely remembered a story that they only cried when they were about to die. Was that true? Or had I imagined it? I could have asked, but their song, if you could call it that, had us both transfixed.

We watched them as they flew past in formation. The pale-bluish January sky behind them was unusually free of clouds. We listened to their wails as they disappeared across the estuary. Shortly after that, we said our goodbyes, my brother and I.

I drove a hundred and sixty-six miles away from the sea.

The 'removals' began the following day, so we realised later. At first, they seemed like strange coincidences. In the county of Carmarthenshire alone, ten people had disappeared during the night. And when I say disappeared, I mean exactly that. They had left in such a way that the dents of their elbows were still there on soft cushions, their slumbering bodies still imprinted on mattress-toppers. 'You'll switch everything off, won't you, dear?', one wife had asked her husband. She had woken at 3am to find the lights still on and some noisy foreign film with subtitles and car crashes lighting up the living room. The doors were shut and the keys still inside. The windows were curtained and closed. The 'remote' was on the sofa arm. But Reg was gone. And so was Philippa from Reigate and Derek from Frome and Emma Barton from Moreton-in-Marsh.

The initial media reaction was uncharacteristically cautious. There was some logical explanation. An armed gang. Fraudulent tax evasion. Organised mass hysteria by a hitherto undiscovered religious sect. More information came to light. Overnight, twenty-one in Cambridge, ten in Norwich, fourteen in central London. And then, as the rest of the world began to wake up, so too in Boston, Kansas City and San Jose. This wasn't a UK phenomenon.

In one 24-hour period, 34,000 people, or thereabouts, had disappeared from the face of the earth. The television schedules were rearranged to accommodate longer current affairs programmes. That evening's newsreader was more solemn than usual. Small scraps of paper kept being handed to her by unidentified hands. A helpline for worried relatives was launched.

The following day, the same thing happened. The police were inundated. The A&E wards were being mobbed by worried relatives convinced that their loved ones must have wandered out in a trance and somehow found themselves on the emergency wards. Even sensible people started talking about supernatural events. It was too odd to be a 'normal' occurrence.

There must be something behind it. People, it was decided, were not just disappearing. They were being 'removed'. Some thing, some power or force that no one understood was taking them away. The experts on that evening's programme debated. It's a dormant cult that's come out into the open. People have cleverly covered their tracks. Ridiculous, others argued. Far too co-ordinated. Rays from outer space. 'They' are vaporising people in their beds. The audience laughed, a little too hysterically I thought. Someone said, sensibly, 'But there's no ash! There are no telltale remains.'

We had news of an immediate survey. Everyone, under penalty of something nasty but unspecified, was expected to complete an online questionnaire. The authorities needed to detect a pattern. Social media filled up with video clips. Look here! This is where she was! You can almost see the dent of her hand on the cushion! We put flour on the carpet... (surely not?) and there's no trail! No footprint! Aliens, someone said. Ridiculous! We imagined teeth and twirly tentacles. Don't be silly, someone else replied. Aliens aren't invisible. They leave trails of goo.

Each morning, there would be the daily updates. Morning television started running out of red pins with which to mark victims' locations. Then, one morning, there was a gloomy announcement. 'We're sorry,' they said. 'Toby, who's been doing the map, was removed last night. We'll do our best to find another pin-sticker-onner.'

Until then, it was like any other disaster. Misfortunes always seemed to happen to someone else's aunty or cousin or colleague that you once shared an office with five years ago. Then, the woman who ran the bakers disappeared. Then, our neighbour's wife. All of a sudden, the 'removed' became known to us. They became familiar. Every day there were more. We rang our children every morning. We messaged them constantly.

Things entered a new phase. It was decided that no one had disappeared from under anyone's nose. People ganged together. They formed sleep clubs. They would take it in turns to stay vigilant. No one would be removed under their watch. That was the theory. But all it took was a sleepy blink of an eye, or a sideways glance. Another one was gone. Families of the 'removed' tried to take 'sleep guardians' to court. They'd been negligent in their duties of care. People chanted on courtroom steps. They held placards. 'That's all very well,' said the courtroom liaison officer in a blaze of flashlights, 'but the judge was removed last night. Case is adjourned.' The sleep clubs were disbanded.

The questionnaires flooded back and were analysed. The rich, the poor, the important, the weak, the strong – no one was safe. Whatever was doing the 'removing' was no respecter of colour or politics or bank statements. The poorer counties claimed that they were suffering greater numbers of removals. The figures disagreed.

Things began to get hysterical. Everywhere, people seemed to be shouting and screaming at everyone else. People who had got used to blaming someone else for all the things that went wrong in their lives were beside themselves. Someone was definitely to blame. And when they found out who they were, there would be hell to pay. They would be lined up against a wall and be made to suffer horribly for inflicting such pain on them, personally. How dare they?

Then, suddenly, it was like a long chain which had been stretched too far. The links that had held fast for so long just popped. The joints opened up and the whole thing sprang apart. The people that had held our world together – the last baker, the last bus driver, the last postman – all of a sudden, they were gone. It didn't matter if you were rich or famous, influential and had thousands of friends on Facebook, what mattered was whether you knew how to fix a generator, or get the car started. It only slowly occurred to us that even if you could get the car started, soon there would be no petrol. And even if there was petrol, from some far-flung depot, the man who drove the lorry would soon be gone.

We rang our children and pleaded with them to come 'home'. But it was already too late. The trains weren't running. No matter, we said, we'll walk. 'Mum, when was the last time you walked a hundred and eight miles? There are looters! Maybe murderers!' They were right. At least, there were looters. To start with. Then even the looters realised that no one with half a brain wanted Rolex watches any more. What we wanted was someone who had flour and who remembered how to bake a loaf. We rang our children and said, 'This might be the last time. We hear the electricity is going.' 'We'll be alright,' they said. 'Will you and Dad be okay?' 'It will stop soon,' we replied. The following day, the power was down, so there was no more landline. We managed one last call to the oil supplier's answerphone before the mobile phone gave up.

'We should have charged it overnight,' I said feebly.

'It was going to go eventually,' you said.

'But we could have said goodbye to the kids,' I cried, or rather, wailed.

'You said goodbye yesterday. And the day before.' It occurred to me that I had married a really heartless man. You were in shock. I realise that now.

'How will we know if they're okay?' I wailed some more.

'You're not going to know,' you said. 'You'd better get used to it. We're not going to know anything any more. We just have to go from day to day. It's all we have. Maybe they're already gone.'

'Who?'

'The kids.'

I was speechless.

The world became surprisingly quiet. The last few cars owned by people who'd stockpiled fuel stopped running. There were no pilots, no planes. The air traffic control had lost all their trained staff. There were no policemen and surprisingly little crime. We'd been given some seed potatoes by the farmer next door before he disappeared. We planted them by hand because his tractor had run out of diesel. Amazingly, they grew, so that winter wasn't too bad. I'd been reading my cookbooks for using our glut of gooseberries. I made tons of jam. But then, although the gooseberries kept on coming, I ran out of sugar. I came across a recipe for fondant mushrooms with glacé cherry mousse and a white wine jus. I laughed so much I gave myself an asthma attack. I laughed some more. Then I started to cry.

'I can't eat gooseberries without sugar,' you said. You'd always loved your food. I'm sure that was the point at which you gave up. I don't think THEY could have realised it, but it was pretty good timing from your point of view.

When I woke the next day I could have sworn I heard you sigh with relief. Another morning, successfully arrived at, I thought.

'Cup of incredibly weak tea?' I joked in the November half-light. But you didn't answer. I turned to face you and the duvet was still warm and shaped around you, but hollowed out.

'Graham?' I said, but I knew you weren't there. I sat for a long while by your side of the bed, stroking the shape of the bedding gently, willing it to stay in your shape.

I couldn't sleep in our bed after that. I couldn't bear the thought of disturbing your shape, the void in the duvet. Over time the shape caved in. The months dragged on. Out on the side of our hill, seven miles from town, there was no sign of anyone any more. No cars had passed for over a year. I tried the electricity from time to time, in the vain hope that something had happened, that civilisation had somehow got back on its feet. But there was nothing.

I planted potatoes. I harvested potatoes. I walked as far as I dared in a day to gather anything that grew, anything I could propagate. I learned to cook on the log burner or ate things raw. I grew peas and worked my way through the stockpile of gooseberry jam. One evening, for supper, I had half a baked potato with boiled peas in a gooseberry jam jus. I used the pages from the fancy cookbooks to keep the fires going. The two most important things were keeping warm and eating. The hedges grew tall and unkempt which was a good thing, I realised. For parts of the year they were full of blackberries, rosehips and sloes. Without pesticides, the mushrooms came back to the fields. A mushroom cooked in wood ash is surprisingly tasty.

I took a perverse pleasure in seeing my neighbour's garden fill up with tasty baby nettles and docks. A space that had seemed under daily attack from power tools and chemicals breathed a sigh of relief, filled out and came back to life. The butterflies, the bees, the fox returned. What had been a sterile lawn was now pockmarked with a wonderful array of molehills. Some mornings, I'd go out there just to count the new mounds. It wasn't all bad.

On my long walks, looking for firewood and food, I would think of the kids, I would think of my brother. Now and again when it all got too much, I'd sit on your side of the bed and talk to what was left of your shape in the duvet. I hoped that wherever you were it wasn't too painful.

Four years had gone by and there had been no signs of life. One day, I ventured to the nearest town. Weeds were growing on the main street. The drainpipes had filled with leaves and some had collapsed. A few shop fronts had been boarded up but in other ways it seemed surprisingly untouched. People had gone quickly, it seemed, before there was too much chaos. The dogs must have gone too, I realised. I had imagined dangerous bloodthirsty packs. Perhaps they'd all been put down as an act of kindness? Perhaps THEY liked dogs? I looked for what I could but there was nothing left. Hardly a match.

I was convinced that I would have been noticed that day. I was fully prepared not to wake up the following morning, or find myself in some strange place full of weird sounds and blue flashing lights. But I woke in the spare bed as usual and when I opened my eyes, I realised with clarity and some degree of dismay, that that was it. Whatever had removed everyone else did not intend to come back for me. I felt strangely betrayed.

Things were getting very bare. In my tiredness, I had let the fire go out. I scoured the house for paper to help me light it. I was down to my last match. I couldn't afford to let it go out again. I had whittled my books down to the essential few, poetry, vegetable gardening and DIY. All the others had gone on the fire. I emptied a drawer and realised to my joy that I had lined it with a copy of the Guardian from years before. I looked at the date. A week after the first removals. There were long discussions on various theories, and then the results of the first questionnaire analysis. I took out the newspaper and scrunched it into a ball. At the door to the log burner, I hesitated. Perhaps this was the last written record? In generations to come, when none of the technology could be made to work, this might be the last piece of evidence. The story of the demise of the human race was about to disappear into my fire. But I had to keep warm.

Very carefully, I lit the last match. I held it to the edge of a page. The word 'swan' glared out at me from the crumpled mass. I poked the ball with a twig. 'I saw swans,' said the sentence. I put my hands in the burner to disentangle the page. I tried to flatten it without stopping the flames. 'Man sees seven swans,' said the headline, and my hands went cold. 'Mr Hopkins from Stirling insists that this is of some importance, given recent events. However, the Prime Minister, interviewed on Radio 4, says that there are no resources to pursue this line of enquiry.' There was more to the interview, but the flame curled around the paper. I poked again and the flame stuttered. I stood back, fearing that I would make the fire go out. I placed thin twigs and wiry branches around the sheet then peered again.

'Believe me,' says Mr Hopkins, 'this has some significance. The point is, you're all asking the wrong questions.' The paper erupted in flames and the twigs crackled. The report was gone. I should have been glad that the fire had taken hold, but all I could think of was that I had destroyed the one clue that might have made a difference. Had the swans really been that important? Was that why I was still here? In which case, was my brother still by the sea, living like me, stockpiling wood and surviving off potatoes and some variety of jam? Was Mr Hopkins still in Stirling?

The evening closed in. I fed the fire its rations. I thought about my children and found myself hoping that they might have noticed the birds. It was unlikely. They hardly looked up from their devices. I blamed myself for their irrelevant, competitive education. I asked myself seriously when was the last time I had walked a hundred and sixty-six miles to the coast. But if, by some miracle, my children had noticed something, they might walk all the way here only to find me gone. What then? I sat by your side of the bed and plumped up the duvet in an attempt to create your shape. I asked you so many questions but didn't get any answers.

That evening I baked a small potato in the burner. I imagined cheese and butter then wondered, what had happened to all the cows? By the light of the fire, I fixed the holes in my socks and sewed patches on my jeans. I needed to get ready for some kind of journey, I was sure of that. But which one? I'd make my decision in the morning, I decided. After a good night's sleep.

Dana Miltins

Dana Miltins is a writer and actor from Melbourne, Australia. For the past twelve years she's been a core artist with one of Australia's leading experimental theatre companies, The Rabble, who are known for their feminist re-imaginings of familiar stories. After graduating from RMIT's esteemed Professional Writing and Editing program, Dana discovered a natural fit with screenwriting. She co-created a TV mini-series The Golden Breed, and web series Soapfiend, which is currently in production. And for something completely different, Dana's currently working on a YA novel.

You Are Here

They're staying in a caravan, for a bit: *She* and *He*. A bed at one end and a built-in air con that's been fighting a losing battle since the eighties. The old caravan opens onto a tin-roofed annex: shade cloth wrapped around the supporting posts for walls, a flyscreen door and paving stone floor. An offcut of carpet designates lounge from kitchen. An armchair, once beige, is rust-coloured from the dust – so are their sneakers, and the sheets, and the washing on the line. You learn to live with it, same as the flies.

Not far down the road is the tip, which they call Bunnings. The twenty (or so) caravans in the park are evolving arthouse palaces, renovated with the refuse of the five-star resort that's a few kay down the road in the place called Town. Kara and Sandy have threaded an ironing board with fairy lights and hung it upside down from their roof to make a chandelier. Barb and Les keep their cutlery in a red metal toolbox. And Lindsay has dropped different kinds of lizards into jars of metho and displayed them on a milk crate bookshelf.

Beyond the caravan park the desert reaches into forever. Facing west Kata Tjuṯa and Uluṟu rise like breaching whales on a red ocean. They say this whole place was once an inland sea, which is hard to imagine now because it's Summer and even the Muṯitjulu waterhole is a pan of cracked earth.

He came here a few months ago, for a job: 'outback resort seeks night security officer, no experience necessary'. He liked the idea of something different, easy. He liked the idea of being alone. He wanted to try out the world without her. To see. He'd told her it was an opportunity to save. For a house, maybe. For the two of them.

For three months she stayed in their half-empty flat. She did girls' nights and detox diets. But the smell of him was still in the cupboard and she found herself standing in there sometimes with his winter clothes and the door closed. She doesn't have time to start all over again. She wants a baby, and soon.

And so she arrived unannounced on an afternoon right before Christmas. For a 'holiday', or at least that's what she told her friends. This was (absolutely) the most wild and romantic thing she had ever done. On the flight, she'd imagined exactly how it would go. The way she would stand. The words she would say. The casual, cool tone of it all. From there she had imagined his unmistakable look, and a whole spectrum of sex positions. It would be a story to tell, one day. 'You were made in a caravan, in the middle of nowhere…'

In reality, however, a wasp had ruined everything. A wasp like a huge airborne mouse – like nothing she had ever seen before. He opened the flyscreen to her cowering on the doormat with her hands covering her head. 'Get away from me'. These were not the words she had practiced.

'What are you doing here?'

This was not the tone she'd imagined. His bare torso, rounder than it used to be, told the story of a life without her. Of toast and beer.

All day he sleeps. All night he works. There is no going outside for outside is like a vast, intolerable sauna and so in daylight hours they lie naked between the air con and the fan. Cabin fever is setting in and her restlessness makes him crazy. He needs to sleep but he can't sleep for the extra heat in the bed, and the hands that wander across his skin. Between her fingers and the bugs, he is always swatting at something.

It has been four days since her arrival and they have made love only once. This is not because she has not been trying but because her trying is unattractive. 'If you'd stop pushing me,' he says, 'you're always pushing me.' He can sense what she's doing. He knows what she wants. But the truth is he never thought she would come here, and he already has two children to his last girlfriend and all he knows of them is that they cost him a hundred and fifty dollars a week. That's an entire shift right there.

He gets up and gets dressed for work. She gets up and boils him two eggs with white bread toast cut into soldiers. The sunset makes the whole world orange. There is so much beauty in this place. She can see it but she can't feel or understand it. There is a list of emergency numbers pinned to the rusty fridge by a magnet that has a picture of space on it. Millions of tiny white stars and a pointer to one of them that says, 'YOU ARE HERE'. This, she feels and understands. She is a speck. A fleck of sand in an endless desert. So close to nothing.

When he leaves for work he reminds her to take a torch if she goes out. She takes it as a sign of his love. But she's afraid to go out alone. The caravan is enclosed and off the ground, and last night she sprayed around the windows and the door. She takes a box of Just Right and eats it in bed, dry. In her imagination, she redecorates: a rug, new sheets (those linen ones), and an Aboriginal painting above the bed.

At midnight she wakes, drenched in sweat and needing the toilet. The block is only twenty metres down the row but she dreads leaving the caravan. She takes the torch from next to the bed and shines a light on each step before taking it. She approaches the flyscreen door knowing that just beyond, out in the world, there is a small huntsman that spends its nights on the doormat. The regularity of its position and the fact that he has named it, like a dog, has so far saved its life. Killing Rex, she feels, would be to admit failure and she won't do that. The light finds the spider, but something is different tonight. Rex's front legs and head are raised. She lets the beam follow the direction of Rex's viewpoint and the light catches the long brown body laid out across the path. Instinct causes her to scream, then run. She slams the flyscreen door, bolts up the caravan steps, slams the caravan door, and falls onto the floor with her heart lifting the skin off her chest. A snake.

In the presence of a snake stand still and silent. This is what she has been told. In stillness you pose no threat, but how to remember that in the moment? She has done the wrong thing. It feels like a test and she has failed. She wants to cry but she has to pee, so bad. Think. Think. There's packet of pads with her toiletries in the milk crate. She unwraps six of them placing them next to each other on top of a plastic bag. Holds up her T-shirt and squats. The relief. She looks up at the ceiling and begins to cry. The universe is sending her a sign, she thinks. It has all been one big mistake, coming here. She isn't cut out for this... place. She will clean up her piss, she will call the snakecatcher, and then tomorrow she will book a flight home. She gathers up the plastic bag around the wet pads, opens the caravan door and races for the emergency numbers under the YOU ARE HERE magnet.

The snakecatcher's troopy pulls up in ten. She calls to him from the top step of the caravan. 'I'm in here'. His steps are close to silent but she tracks the beam of his torch around the shade cloth to the flyscreen door. He's in dusty denim and old Air Jordans. He looks exactly as a snakecatcher should look: cool and sure. 'Where is it?' he asks. His smile glows in the dark.

'It's right over there somewhere.'

She steps down from the caravan, to take hold of his forearm, which could rival her thigh in width. 'Somewhere there', she says, holding onto him tighter. The snakecatcher raises his torch. The snake is meandering up the path, unfazed, towards the block. The snakecatcher hands her the torch and his special snakecatching bag that looks something like a heavy-duty butterfly net. 'Only a python,' he says. 'Not deadly.'

As silent and fluid as the snake itself, the snakecatcher moves in behind the python. Sensing his presence, the snake pauses, turns to look back, questioning this interruption. The snakecatcher is fast and gentle. He reaches for the tail, catches it and stands up, raising his arm so that the snake dangles free from the ground. It is helpless now, this beautiful length of striped brown muscle. It must be close to two metres long and she'd be lucky to reach her two hands around its middle. The snakecatcher strokes the belly of the snake with his free hand and says something to it in a language that she cannot understand. Then he lifts the snake to cradle it in his arms.

Fertility snake,' he says, 'Kuniya.' In his culture, sacred. He points out the tiger stripes and the size of its head and all the while Kuniya is moving slowly through his arms and hands, enjoying his touch as if they're casual lovers. He takes the handle of the bag from her and lowers Kuniya in. On its way down, he lets her touch the smooth pale belly. She holds the bag for him while he ties it shut; she is astounded by the weight. She wants to know what will happen. He explains that he will drive far enough away and let Kuniya go. She offers him a beer first.

In Tjukurpa, the Python Woman, Kuniya, lived far away to the east of Uluru but when it came time for her to have babies she wanted them to be born in the same sacred place where she had been born. So she carried her eggs around her neck, travelling for days across the desert to a cave at Uluru where she carefully laid them down.

Kuniya is in the bag on the lounge-room floor between them, unmoving, asleep maybe. She believes she can feel Kuniya's energy. It seeps into her. She too has come a long way to this place.

When Kuniya heard that her nephew had been speared by a group of poisonous snake men, she left the cave to search for him. The Liru men had fled towards Kata Tjuṯa, except for one. When Kuniya asked about her nephew, he laughed. And so Kuniya begun a ritual dance, picking up the earth and putting it on herself: drawing its power, harnessing her rage. She struck the Liru man with her wana, killing him; and then she carried the body of her nephew to the Muṯitjulu waterhole where they were transformed into waṉampi.

At sunrise, *He* returns from his shift to find a parade of empty beer bottles on the lounge room floor. It was his beer. He bought it. He opens the fridge to check exactly how much of his fresh slab is gone. Half. That's fifty bucks out here. He knows she is capable of two, maybe three, on a good night, which leaves nine unaccounted for. He yanks open the caravan door. It's stifling hot inside and there's a smell about the place. She's alone in the bed, damp and twisted, like the sheets. He gives her a shove. Her eyelids flicker. He pulls at the sheet and she groans. 'Who were you with?' he wants to know. She flexes her fingers, working her way out of a dream.

There is a glass of water on the bedside table. He picks it up and dumps it over her face. Her eyes open to a spinning, spluttering world. 'What are you doing?' she says.

'Who were you with?' he wants to know.

She tries to sit herself up but he pushes down on her chest with his hands, holding his weight on her. 'Who were you with?'

'Ouch' she cries out. 'No one. I wasn't with anyone.'

She tries to explain. There was a snake and then a snakecatcher. He stayed for a beer and they talked. 'That's it. He's a friend. You wanted me to make friends.'

It makes him laugh that she could be so stupid.

'It's not like that,' she says.

But, there's something lost about the way he's laughing. The way his laughter seems to turn inwards. He's gone somewhere, even though he's right there pushing on her chest.

Her stomach rises into her throat, beer and Just Right, but she holds on, reaches out for him. 'Baby, please, listen.' He stands up and steps away from her catching his heel in the cord of the fan, which crashes to the floor. It lies on its side, the blades whining, until he kicks it enough to make them stop. 'I HATE THIS FUCKING THING.' Then he slams the caravan door. Jealousy, she thinks, could be a good sign.

It is six-thirty in the morning and he is going to have one of his beers that he bought. He makes his way to the kitchen knocking an empty over on his way and a whole line of them topple like dominoes. The clatter of glass splits open the silence, and on the lounge-room floor a bag, like a heavy-duty butterfly net with the top tied off with a piece of rope, begins to move of its own accord. It catches his eye.

Out the back of the caravan park there's a small clearing: a square of red dust with a lone desert oak at one end. The tree would be close to a thousand years old. It has seen the world change and now it has a basketball hoop nailed into its trunk. Sometimes he comes out to play but today he dumps a shovel and the bag in the dust. He takes off his shirt. Skin burnt deep red: a flesh singlet. He takes a long swig of beer and then for kicks pours some over the bag. 'You like that?'

The bag writhes, which makes him laugh in that strange internal way. Then he places his beer in the sand and takes up the shovel. Raising it above his head, he brings the shovel down on the Python Woman. Again. Again. Again. Until the bag is dead still. Until a brown-red liquid seeps through the canvas. And then again. And again. To be sure. The Kuniya is gone. Then he sits in the dust and finishes his beer.

It takes Her a little while to raise herself. She is hung over and in no state to deal with one of his temper tantrums. She looks around at this life: her bag in the corner (still unpacked), the clothes rack (a piece of pipe hitched between two lamp stands), the mismatched polyester sheets. What was clear last night has become foggy. Right now, all she wants is a cup of tea and food so she steps down from the caravan into the annex. She puts the kettle on the stove and she places eggs in a saucepan of water to boil.

When he returns she is drinking tea, stuck somewhere between staying and going. She'd like to be the person who just packs up and leaves, but she's the person who makes breakfast and initiates a conversation. The kitchen table is set. Salt and pepper, and toast cut into dipping soldiers. But they'll be useless now, he's taken so long to return that her eggs are overdone. He drops the bag at her feet and sits down to watch as she takes it in: all the brown blood. 'You don't need to be afraid,' he says, 'I killed it.'

Martin Pevsner

Martin Pevsner is a writer of novels and short stories. He is as interested in form as in content. In his writing he finds himself exploring themes of family, friendship, childhood, love, isolation, age, memory, fear, loss, death and the pursuit of happiness. He was born in London but has lived in Norwich, Manchester and Bristol in UK. He has also lived in Cameroon, Zimbabwe and Namibia and has travelled widely around the African continent. Since 1997 he has lived and worked in Oxford. He is currently studying on a part-time MA in Creative Writing at Oxford Brookes.

There's a Place

You've forgotten something, now what was it? You park beside a hatchback and let the engine idle while you gather your thoughts. It's stopped spitting so you flip off the wipers. You peer through the fog-filmed windscreen. A leaden sky, low and close like the first day of the end.

This is the place you come to when you've something on your mind, a dilemma to weigh, a knot to unravel. An hour's drive but a world away. No concrete and neon, no traffic fumes and dog mess. No thumpthump beat from passing cars, no fastfood reeks and no half-eaten kebab to line the gutters.

The makeshift carpark lies encircled by a wilderness, a siege of hazel and hawthorn, beech and brambled sycamore. You reach over to the passenger footwell for your hiking boots and waterproof trousers, swing your legs out onto the puddled gravel and begin dressing. Winter coat and hat and gloves. You slip your binoculars over your head, shut the car door and flip the locking switch on your key fob.

As you amble towards the footpath you meet a man your age, pebbledash hair and ruddy cheeks in waxcloth jacket and mud-streaked wellingtons.

"Wet enough for you?"

You have no slick response, smile by way of answer and nod and pass.

Now you're alone. There's a hedgerow on your right, skeletal hawthorn pitted with berries not yet picked over by fieldfare and redwing. Past blackthorn and damson, a writhing wall of spike and spine. On the other side, the brackish ditch and barbed fence separates path from meadow, a wetland peppered with Canada geese and scatterings of rook and crow.

Up ahead there are the willows where volunteers hang feeders filled with nuts for finches and tits, and where squirrel and pheasant visit to pick up the spillings. You and Shula used to take Millie here in the buggy and together you'd count the greenfinch, one two three. Sometimes a woodpecker would appear, a flash of scarlet amongst the muted foliage, and Millie would point and squeal and coo. You wish you'd had a place to come to like this when you were Millie's age.

When you were Millie's age, you knew nothing of wildlife beyond picture books and cartoons on the television. The only greenery was your local park where your mother sometimes took you. You picture yourself running through puddles in bright red wellies. There was a slide and a seesaw. There would have been birds and squirrels but you never noticed.

It was later, at university in Wales, that your interest was first pricked. A day trip to the seaside, a coastal path walk with housemates, one of them a birder armed with binoculars, pointing out chough and peregrine and raven. After that you got hold of a book, studied the glossy pictures, bought your first pair of bins.

There's a young couple with three children at the feeder today, and the usual assortment of songbirds. A small blonde girl in pink trainers, sated with birdlife, turns and eyes you enquiringly.

"Why's that man walking funny, Mummy?"

The mother turns and you watch her embarrassment surge and peak. You smile to show your understanding, feel her discomfort as she struggles to formulate a response. You pass on, unwilling to hear the answer.

You turn left beyond the feeders and now you're on the bridle path. On your right, a reed-flanked stream separates the path from meadowland. On the left lies a strip of wetland wood, willow and alder and birch. The strip has been flooded once and once again these past months, fallen logs furred in moss, the ground a patched carpet of liverwort and lichen. You peer through the foliage and freeze. A muntjac, skittish, pauses its foraging, snuffles your scent and vanishes in the mist. A moment to savour. You haven't seen one of those here for years, not since you first came with Shula.

You first came with Shula when you began courting. It was just along from this spot, a late spring Sunday. You heard the tender purr of a turtle dove, traced it to the branch of an oak tree. Shula, a newcomer to birding, thought it was enchanting. Later you walked as far as Sedgley Compton and somewhere on the way, in a copse that smelled of mulch and mushroom, you spotted the muntjac. Soon after that you lay down for a rest and one thing led to another. At intimate moments together, you like to speculate that it was there that Millie was conceived.

Your pet names for each other originate from that period, from your growing interests in plant – and wildlife respectively: Flora and Fauna. Although your own nickname never took off, you've often called her Flo. No one else does. It's like a codeword, secret and intimate.

Now you gaze out onto the meadow. In the distance a clustering of lapwing, blunt-winged and crested, take to the air and spin and fall. You remember a description you read once, how they rose and settled like windblown newspaper. Now where did that come from?

You feel a pressing urge to pee. Damn this dodgy bladder. You glance around but the coast is clear. You relieve yourself against a fence post and zip yourself up.

A song has infiltrated, a tune from your past. It's been with you all day, you wonder what triggered it. You concentrate, play with the few bars you've been humming, let it swirl around your head like wine on a palate until, there it is, the penny drops. Yes, it's a Beatles song, an early one. Sweet and wistful, a hint of melancholy. You bought the LP when it first came out, washed neighbours' cars for weeks, saved up your money. You can't have been more than twelve years old. You wonder where the record is now. You lost your LP collection in dribs and drabs over the years. What about your record player? Yes, now you remember. You cleared out the spare bedroom. It must have gone to the council dump. That was just when Millie was born.

When Millie was born, after she'd been weighed and measured and counted, after she'd been washed and fed and laid up against Shula's breast, her eyes shut and her lips puckered, a dribble of breastmilk on her chin. After Shula had drank her tea and eaten the chocolate you'd packed in her hospital bag, and assured you for the fifth time that she was fine, she'd like to sleep a little please. After you walked out of the ward and along the striplit corridors and emerged to a bright February dawn, you felt a sudden spasm, tremendous, a protestation as your metabolism rebelled against the lack of sleep, the exhaustion, the nerves, the cup after cup of vending coffee on empty stomach. And you stumbled over to the gutter and knelt and retched and retched, steaming coffee and stringy bile and lumps of clotted mucous. And when there was nothing left, you stood up and wiped your mouth with your sleeve and realised that the worst was over, you now felt better, better than you'd ever felt before.

That song's still playing in your head. You wonder what triggered it. You're trudging down the bridle path now, heading for the first hide. In the summer this is your favourite spot. The grass is longer during that season and as you traipse, with every step, butterflies will take flight, common blue and meadow brown. At that time of year the sumptuous reeds are alive with warblers, the meadow criss-crossed by darting hobbies that quarter and swoop for dragonfly between post-top breaks.

No butterflies today. No summer migrants resting up from their African odyssey. Today it's a place for the hardy. Or perhaps the foolish, you think. Even with gloves your hands are icy. In your hurry to leave the house, you must have forgotten to eat and now you are hungry. Your mouth is dry and you dig around in your pocket, pull out a packet of mints. Mmm, that's the ticket. Far off in the distance, kite and buzzard ride the skyline thermals.

Up ahead you see a man in camouflage trousers and woolly hat. He has a long-lensed camera on a tripod that he's aimed at a thicket of blackthorn. As you approach, he turns and you see his face clearly for the first time, a stubbled chin and close set eyes and mouth set in a frown.

"Seen any brambling?" he asks without preamble. A smoker's voice, tight and rasping.

You shake your head. There's a frustration in the man's tone that makes you wish you'd seen one, if only to please him.

"Two days on the trot I've been here and nothing to show for it," he adds in a way that sounds to you as if someone, you or the bramblings perhaps, were to blame, an act of negligence or spite.

"Well, good luck," you manage.

Another thirty yards and you reach the hide. A short stop here, it's part of your ritual. You climb the steps and open the door.

Inside the wooden structure, three young men in one corner are admiring the winter flocks of linnet and chaffinch and reed buntings. You glance through the window, spot a yellowhammer in the hawthorn, a neon buzz amongst the grey. A moment later a pink-chested bullfinch, blackcapped and beefy, alights on the branch of a yew.

Across in the far corner, gazing out at the floodplain, a middle-aged couple are eating sandwiches from a tupperware box. You breathe in through your nose and gather the faint whiff of fishpaste. Damn, you think. Why didn't you bring a packed lunch? And when the woman takes a thermos from her backpack and pours out a mug of tea, you realise you didn't even bring your flask. Silly old fool, you think. You never forget your flask. You stand with your hands in your pockets, feel the tube of mints, pull one out as consolation.

The confectionary is comforting. As you suck, your tongue probes the gap where you had the molar pulled on the upper right side, how long ago was that? An indelible imprint: the dentist's chair, the white ceiling, the classical music in the background. The pliers, Mr Singh's grunts of effort. That's a memory you'd be happy to forget.

That was a milestone in your ageing process, you think. Like the colon surgery and the stroke. When you were twenty, you thought you'd live forever. You never thought you'd meet someone for keeps. You never thought you'd get married, have a child, get a mortgage. You never thought you'd get flat feet and piles and have a stroke and a tooth pulled and some of your colon removed. You never even thought you'd get a steady job and you certainly never believed there'd be a time when you were sixty-five and up for retirement.

When you were sixty-five and up for retirement, they held a party for you at the head office. David Osbourne made a speech and there was a presentation. It was summer, the office windows were open. They set up a buffet with drinks and people spilled out onto the courtyard. You wandered out, tipsy on fizzy wine, and from a distance you watched the Scottish girl from Accounts and the caretaker lad, what was his name? Lou? Luke? He made a joke and she smiled and touched his arm, and you felt an ache somewhere between grief and joy.

You leave the hide, pass over the stile and take the winding footpath that leads down to the water's edge. You leave billows of breath in your wake as you amble. There are reedbeds on one side, farmer's land on the other. Here, squeezed between pasture and water, is Shula's favourite spot in spring, where she hunts the verges for shepherd's needle and corncockle, broad-leaved spurge and pheasant's-eye. And sometimes you'll come off the path and walk across the grassland, and along the edges she'll spot green-winged orchids and pepper saxifrage and adder's-tongue fern while you look for meadow pipit and skylark and wary brown hare.

Your thoughts are interrupted by the appearance of a bearded man in navy anorak and dogtooth cap. A broad smile, an open face. A moment's panic as you wonder whether you know him, then you realise that's just his manner.

"Lovely day for it," he offers by way of an opening.

"Yes," you answer.

"Going down to the screen?"

"Yes. Seen much there?"

The man considers the question.

"The marsh harriers are out. Plenty of widgeon, teal, tufties. That north wind's a bit nippy though. It's coming in straight off the water. Weather for thermals and a hip flask, eh?"

He smiles again, inviting you to laugh and you do so, a chuckle of sorts.

"Well, good luck," he says and passes on.

The screen shelter is empty and you peer through the viewing slots at the expanse of reed-fringed water. Amongst all the ducks, a cormorant stands on a mudbank, its wings spread like a giant, sinister bat. You scan the far side with your binoculars. There's a heron out there fishing, its body frozen, poised for the spearing thrust into the slategrey sheen. Behind it half a dozen snipe are huddled at the water's edge. The place looks, this winter's day, like primordial swamp from the Paleolithic period, and the impression is reinforced when you catch a glimpse, a split-second instant, of a bittern in flight, just a moment's glimpse before it swoops and falls, like an ancient pterodactyl, behind an atoll of marshy canes.

It's wonderful luck, only the second time you've seen bittern here, and you scan the reeds for a second view. Nothing. The wind is picking up now. Funnelled through the viewing windows, it cuts you to the bone. You'd like to stay a while longer – you haven't seen the marsh harriers yet – but without your flask and woolly thermals, you're shivering now. Once more you curse yourself for your forgetfulness.

The elation carries you back to the main hide, back along the bridle path, past the hanging feeders. You'd like to meet another soul, share your good fortune, pass on the tip for someone else to catch a glimpse, but the pathways are empty save for robins and dunnock that peck at the ground before you, then flutter up to the hedgerows to watch your ungainly passing.

Now you feel the urge to pee again. Bloody bladder. You glance around. This time you're relieved to be alone. You press yourself into a hedge and go about your business. This almost permanent need to pee, it's another sign of ageing, like the tooth and the colon and all. This you ponder, but now, still jubilant at the bittern sighting, your outlook is more serene, almost chipper. You're a lucky man, you think. You've had a great game. You're well into the second half now and there's not much more to hope for but injury time and the final whistle. But still, you can't complain.

You pause on the home stretch to gaze out over the blackthorn. Once, at this time of year, a chap told you he'd seen a hawfinch at this spot and now you scan the trees with your binoculars. That would be the end of a spectacular day, you think. It's not a natural spot for them, they prefer tall deciduous trees. But, well, you never know. They might be tempted by the shrivelled sloes remaining on the branches.

You give it twenty minutes. You're no longer shivering but your hands and feet are numb and your nose has developed a steady drip. You hunt through your pockets for a tissue, wipe yourself as you scan the treetops one last time. You return the sodden Kleenex to your pocket, come upon the tube of mints, pop one into your mouth.

Mmm, you think. Just the ticket.

Now you are back in the car park. For a moment you think your vehicle has gone, but no, it's hidden from view by a hulking Land Rover. As you turn past it, you spot a police car parked next to yours. A female officer is standing beside the driver's door, a policeman gets out of the passenger side. Now a young woman in a beige coat emerges from the back, closes the door, smiles when she sees you. She has blond hair, black-rimmed glasses, soft pale features as if a little out of focus. There's something vaguely familiar about her countenance. The way she brushes a strand of hair from her eyes, the curve of her smile. She reminds you of someone, now who is it?

She walks right up to you, closer than you expect, places a hand on your arm

"Are you OK?" she asks.

"Yes, thank you," you answer. Out of politeness, you add, "How are you?"

"You've been for a wander again. Mum's been really worried."

You don't answer. You have to think about this.

"You left your mobile phone at home again."

You nod. That's probably true. You hesitate, uncertain what happens next. The woman squeezes your arm.

"Let's go home, eh, Dad? I'll drive, shall I? We'll have a nice cup of tea when we get back."

She's leading you to the passenger side of your own car. Once you're seated and belted, she returns to the officers. She's speaking to them now, a brief conversation. You lean back and close your eyes and try to remember where you were. And all that you recall is nothing and all that you've forgotten is everything you lost.

But then you picture the bittern and your heart fills with joy again, and you think, I'll tell her. As soon as she gets inside the car, I'll tell her all about it.

Ian Priestley

Ian Priestley was born and grew up in the Manchester area before leaving to work as a teacher overseas. He has somehow ended up in Japan, which he finds a constant source of inspiration. When not struggling to learn Japanese, he tries to write short stories. His writing has appeared in Asian-based newspapers, magazines and anthologies. He finds he gets his best ideas on long train journeys.

The Road Home

I have been a walker all my life. Even when I was too young to walk, my mother carried me on her back and when we stopped at night, I could still feel her footsteps, like a heartbeat inside me.

Today, the sun is shining and our mood has lifted after two days of rain. Someone shouts "God bless you," from the window of a passing car. "A good sign," says Rozen. He keeps telling us that the people in the next town will welcome walkers. He is sure, but he has been sure about other places before. As the sun sets, we find ourselves approaching the outskirts of the town. Some people stand in their gardens and watch us pass. Rozen calls out "Hello." Some nod back, others turn away.

We set up our tents of tarpaulin and plastic sheets in a field by the road. There are about forty of us now. I heard in the past walking groups were bigger, but divided up when they started to be turned away from towns. A few times we have met other groups coming the opposite way.

A police car stops by the camp. Rozen and Anja go and talk to the men in their black uniforms. I don't hear what they say, but the policemen scowl as they speak and one of them takes in the camp with a sweep of the hand and waves it away. Rozen talks. I don't have to listen to know what he is saying. They are haggling for another day or two. He points to me. "Look, we have young ones," he is saying. Soon he will point to Servan.

Old Servan with his stick and stories. I have heard his stories hundreds of times, and sometimes they change with the telling. Servan is from somewhere, he likes to say. He has his homeland, his dialect, the words he sometimes rolls around his mouth like a piece of tough meat. Unlike me. I am from nowhere.

Old Servan and I go into the town. He is the oldest and I am young, about thirteen years old. They tell me I have an innocent face. In town, we stop to look through the window of a supermarket. I watch a woman and a young girl loading food from the trolley into their bags. The daughter sees my face pressed against the glass. I smile at her. She says something to her mother, who looks at me. It is the kind of look people in our group give to stray dogs that come into our camp when a fire burns at night.

I hold a piece of cardboard. On it is written, Please help us. We are tired, hungry.

A couple of boys, younger than me, pass with their mother. One of them holds a string with coloured balloons attached. I see him look at my trousers, tied together with string. The mother wants to go on, but the boy with the balloons pulls at her sleeve. She opens her purse and gives the boy something. He walks back to us and puts a 5 Kro note in Servan's can. I look at the balloons, which strain at the string like dogs on a leash. I want to hold them so I reach for the string. The boy's eyes show fear. He looks back to his mother. She is there; he is safe. He lets go. It is the most wonderful thing to hold these balloons as they tug and flap in the wind. It is like they have some kind of magic in them.

Once we stayed near a fairground. There were painted horses that spun around to music, balloons, the smell of sweet candy, hot dogs, and there was a man with a tattoo of a woman on his arm who let me ride on the waltzers for free as he passed from each carriage, like a bird hopping between branches of a tree. Liza was the name of the woman.

"What happened to her?" I asked.

"She's gone," he said. I understood. Like my mother. People go.

I visited the waltzers every day. At night, the man told stories of his life with the fair. His life was like ours, always moving, but in the fairground there are the rides, the stalls; they have something people want and when the fair comes into a town, people are drawn to the smells, the sounds, the colour – like bees to flowers. We have nothing to attract bees. We only attract stray dogs that shit on our campsite.

"You could stay with me, work on the ride," he said.

Rozen told me not to trust him. "What does he want from you? People always want something," he told me.

"This man, I think he likes young boys," Sabir said, "he wants your little ass." They all laughed, even the women. But they were wrong about the man. He only wanted to talk. He was lonely.

I let the balloons go and they fly into the sky. I watch them rise. When I take my eyes off them, I see the boy's mother looking down at me. "Little rat," she hisses.

Servan is annoyed. "Don't bite the hand that feeds you," he tells me. "Now show me your innocent face, your sad face. Be good. Not a little swine like Jano."

Jano is sixteen. Even when he was young, Servan said, you couldn't take him into town. Nobody wanted to give him any money. He has eyes like a little devil. He makes women want to grab their purses, not open them.

"Good, little Ari," Jano said to me one night. "I need your help."

In the dark, he pointed out a drainpipe that passed a small window. "All you need to do is climb up and pull the window open. It's too small for me, but you can get in and open one of the doors."

I followed Jano from room to room as his torch light found closets and drawers, stopping sometimes to listen for any sound, like a rat going through garbage. One room we came to had a picture of football players on the wall.

"Nothing here, just the kid's room," Jano said. But when he left, I stayed. I understood why he had chosen this house. The family was so rich even children had their own rooms.

There was a bed and I wanted to know how it felt, so I lay back on it. Above the bed, patches of light glowed. As I watched, the patches became groups of tiny lights, and I realised that this child had his own night sky, with stars that somehow shone in the dark, in his bedroom. I imagined this was my bed, and he, not me, lived outside in the fields. But then I remembered summer nights sleeping outside when the real sky seemed so close you felt you were among the stars.

"Are you ready to sleep, little Ari?"

I jumped up. Jano was looking at me, smirking.

"You want me to leave you here in your nice bed?"

I stood and went towards the door. He put his hand on my chest.

"Maybe that's not such a bad idea. Leave you here, and see what they do when they find a new bird in their nest. You want me to do that? Perhaps they will take pity on you and treat you like a son. Just pull a sad face like you do for the old women who give you money."

I don't trust Jano when he is like this. His eyes were mean, spiteful,

"You have such an innocent face, Ari, nobody can resist you."

I tried to pass him, but he pushed me back into the room.

"I'll tell them you made me do it. They will believe me because nobody trusts you. The police will lock you up. Not in a nice room like this, but in a stinking tiny cell, like Astur."

The police came for Astur one night after a fight. Two men had insulted him, Astur said. He ignored them, but they were drunk, told him to go back to where he came from. Astur said nothing. But when the men came to him, he kicked one in the balls and hit the other with his head. His girlfriend and Rozen went to see him in jail. It was small, like an animal cage, they said, and they didn't know when he would be let out. To someone who is used to walking, to have nowhere to walk to is a terrible thing.

Jano called me a little girl, but we left together.

Servan says it has been a good day as he looks in the box. He empties it and we are about to leave when a man and a woman approach. She wears shoes with pointed heels made from the skin of a snake. His are of soft black leather and they shine like a lake in the moonlight. Servan taught me this, to look at the shoes if you want to know if someone has money. The man bends down to look into my eyes and he smiles.

"How old are you, my little friend?" he asks.

"He is only eleven years old," Servan lies.

"So young," says the woman "and such a sweet face. Is his mother not with him?" she asks Servan.

He begins to tell the story of how I was born on the road and how my mother disappeared. "He is from nowhere," says Servan, "and has nothing."

I feel like kicking the old man sometimes. Always they tell me I am from nowhere, but where is this somewhere that the men told Astur to go back to? The older ones remember war, fear, leaving everything behind, but they also remember a time before that. And at night around the fire, they blow on the hot ashes of their memories to keep themselves warm. Rozen remembers his father's farm and lemon trees as far as you could see. Anja remembers the brothers and sister she slept with at night like kittens curled up together. Berkan kept chickens and swam in the lake. Kirsal's mother baked bread that you dipped, still warm, into olive oil. Servan remembers a girl called Sera, almost as beautiful as his own mother, who was the kindest and most beautiful woman in the whole town.

I am tired of the pity of this couple and Servan's stories, so I walk away. The people drinking coffee outside see me and look into their phones. When I go back to Servan, the couple are still there. They stop talking when I approach. The couple smile but I can't read anything behind the smiles. The man passes Servan a card then he bends down and offers me his hand.

"My name is Ivan," he says, "and this is Mira." The woman now puts out her hand. "It was nice to meet you," she says.

On the way back, Servan is quiet.

There was a town near a border. It was summer and we camped near a river. In the mornings, Mum and me would go to the river to wash. She would put her feet in the water. Her toenails were rotten like Servan's teeth, and her heels looked like crusts of bread, so I took them one at a time in my hand and washed them. She looked at me sweetly then.

People came, they brought us bread, fruit, even pies. They took pictures of themselves with us and said they would help. Then the weather turned bad. By the time they came to move us over the border most of the people had stopped coming. But Mum loved that place and didn't want to leave, so when she disappeared I knew that's where she'd gone. I tried to go back but the police stopped me. I asked Servan why she didn't take me and he said it was because she knew I was safe with them and she didn't want to put me in danger. I know she is waiting for me in that town and one day when we pass through again – Servan says that we always return to the same place again in the end – my journey will finish.

"Anything is possible," Sabir said.

"Don't give up hope," Anja told me.

"They're lying to you. She jumped off a bridge," said Jano. But Jano is a lying pig.

That night at the camp I notice the others looking at me and talking.

Something happened and it is to do with the couple with the nice shoes. The next day, Rozen comes and speaks to me, tells me how he is tired of walking and how it is no life for a young boy like me. Wouldn't I like to go to sleep in a nice bed and to have someone to take care of me? I tell him I have a mother and one day I will find her again.

The next morning Jano tells me someone has come to see me. It is the couple, and there is a boy with them. He is younger than me, but dressed like a man in a shirt and tie.

"This is Luka," the man called Ivan says. "He would like to be friends with you, wouldn't you, Luka?" Luka nods, but he doesn't mean it. As I step forward he backs away like a frightened kitten. These town boys are weak and scared.

"Ivan and Mira were worried about you and have come all the way to see you again, Ari. Isn't that kind of them?" Servan says.

They look down at me. The man smiles; the woman shows a pitying face. Rozen shows off to the couple, tells stupid jokes. They laugh. The woman keeps her eye on the boy, who sometimes looks at me, but when I catch his eye, he looks at the ground.

Two days later, the man comes again. This time he is alone. Rozen brings him to me. He shakes my hand. It is a big hand but the skin is soft. He takes Rozen in his car somewhere. The others look at me and whisper. When Rozen comes back, he's been drinking. He has brought more bottles and we are celebrating. When I ask him what we are celebrating, he puts his face in front of mine and I smell the drink on his breath. "You, little Ari," he says, "You."

The next day Rozen invites me to join him and some other members of the group. We sit in a circle. Rozen nods at Sabir. Sabir the storyteller, the talker. "He is full of shit," my mother used to say.

"This life we live is no life at all," he says. "Walking, walking without anywhere to walk to. I curse my life most days." He spreads his arms to include the others. "We all do."

"You are young, so the walking comes easy now... but it is harder as you get older. It wears you out. Not just your body... but here, too." He taps his head. "I know you understand. You saw it in your mother, little Ari."

I feel my fists clench.

"But you know what keeps me going, what keeps me from becoming crazy? What I think about on those days when it rains, or the wind blows so hard it hurts your ears, or those days when they call us dogs, tell us to fuck ourselves and keep moving? When all you want to do is be left by the roadside to die like the old ones, you know what keeps me going?"

I say nothing.

"I remember the home I once had. And I dream that some day I might find one again, and this journey will end. And I will not have to beg for food, or plead with the police to let us stay, or have to pack everything up and start walking again. That's what keeps me going.

But it's different for you Ari. You don't have those memories. You are from nowhere; you have no idea what it is like to belong."

I turn away and see Jano, next to Servan, watching Sabir.

"But now little Ari," Sabir says. "Now you have a chance."

I told them. I have a home. It is waiting for me in the town where my mother is. I reminded Servan of what he had said about always returning to the same place again. Rozen said something under his breath and looked angrily at the old man. This time Jano was watching me.

It is a clear summer's morning and I have a can of fish and a slice of bread. I hear from the others that in a few days we begin to walk again. I am happy about this. I don't want to stay here. I want things to get back to normal and not to see the couple again, so there will be no more looks or questions. I will go into the next town with Servan, and show them such a sweet face they will fill the old man's can with money.

But then Rozen and Servan come for me. Rozen calls me little Ari, and I think everything is back to normal. Then he asks me to go for a walk, and I know that it isn't.

"Servan has something to tell you," he says.

The old man is uncomfortable. He is not going to tell me a funny story or lie about his mother being the most beautiful woman in the town. Instead he tells me about my mother.

"She is not waiting for you in that town," he says. "I am sorry to tell you this, but your mother is dead."

I tell him he is a liar, just like Jano. But then Rozen talks.

"We tried to hide it because we were worried about you. You were so young. But you are old enough to know the truth now, little Ari. She is dead."

I curse them, call them liars.

"So, if she is dead, how did she die?" I ask.

"She killed herself," says Rozen. "She jumped from a bridge."

There is a party for me. Azan plays his guitar and sings old songs about love and being alone. Sabir tells a story of how I will be a great man with education and one day I will have enough money to return and give them all a home. They are sad, but Rozen has bought more alcohol. He shares it with everybody. Soon they forget their sadness. I see Jano on the other side of the bonfire. He is not smiling like the others.

The woman called Mira is holding a string of balloons. I have Servan to thank for this, I think. She waits with the man called Ivan by their car. Rozen, Anja and Servan walk with me. Servan says he will miss me, but we will be sure to meet again soon. Rozen says they will call to make sure everything is okay. Anja pulls me against her chest, and tells me this is what my mother would have wanted. As she holds me, I see Jano coming towards us. He comes closer but Rozen blocks his way.

"They are liars," he says. "All of them. They have sold you, like an animal." His head jerks back. Rozen has him by the arm. He swings him around then hits him in the face with the back of the hand. I hear Jano cursing as I enter the car.

I take the balloons with me out of the car, but the man, Ivan, tells me to let them go. We watch as they drift upwards. "They are free," he tells me, "just like you."

The house stands alone surrounded by fields.

"See, there is plenty of space for you to play with your brothers and sisters. We didn't tell you about your brothers and sisters. We have a big family. But don't worry, you won't be treated any differently. They are all like you. Not real brothers and sisters. You see, Mira and I can't have children." I look at the woman, but she looks away.

I am nervous about the others and want to meet them soon, but they are playing upstairs, Ivan says and he will introduce me to them later. Mira makes me a sandwich with a thick slice of beef and lettuce. The beef is tender and and the flavour so good I eat it quickly, forgetting everything for the moment, just the taste. She brings me a glass of milk, and I am thirsty after the beef, so I drink it in one go. Then I become so tired all I want to do is sleep.

In the dark my mother is crying again. I have asked her often why she cries in the dark, but she won't tell me, or else she denies it in the morning. But I hear her. I reach my hand to touch her back, but then I realise this is not my mother. A boy turns. I look into his eyes. It is the boy named Luka and his eyes are full of fear, but not of me. The cries are not his. There are others. Then someone moves from the corner and in the moonlight I see the man called Ivan standing over me. But this is not the same man as the one who brought me here. This one has the look of the devil in his face and I call for my mother.

Peter Slater

Peter Slater is an English teacher, living in London. Last year, he was a prize winner in the essay competition run by *The London Magazine*. A more recent essay was also published in the same magazine in June of this year. Currently, he is working on a memoir centred on a year he spent working on a farm in the heart of the Queensland rainforest.

Water in the Desert

The place felt wrong from the start. Something had happened here. Or was going to happen. They'd parked in a disused quarry that had been converted into a makeshift truck stop. In the golden, late afternoon light, objects possessed an unnerving clarity. Next to a wooden shack, where a bearded Bedouin sold warm fruit juice, snacks and cigarettes, there was a single rusty petrol pump, topped by a glass dome that said ESSO. A bin overflowed with cans, bottles and crisp packets; a camel sat tied to a wooden stake.

From his safe distance beneath the shelter, with its hanging sign smokas, Edward drew deep on the beautiful cigarette smoke and felt that momentary joy that made addiction so wonderful. He looked over at the rest of the tour party clustered around the coach in small groups. All were afraid to leave the security of metal, engine and the girl soldier who stood smoking, a rifle over her shoulder. The Army, Edward reflected bitterly, was exempt from being sent to the leper colony where he was now exiled. He was also angry at himself for obeying the smoking rule. In the middle of the desert! It had been a miserable journey through the Negev. The air conditioning in the coach had been ferociously cold, giving the sun-scorched scenery outside the tinted windows a sense of unreality. They had passed canyons and gorges, seen mountains and uncanny cratered moonscapes, but it was like watching a tedious documentary that long outstayed its welcome and most of the tourists spent most of their time scrolling on their phones and tablets. He had had small snore-broken lumps of sleep and now a dull headache.

Maria was flumped on the steps of the coach, holding a whirring battery fan close against a face obscured by a floppy-brimmed hat. Her white blouse was damp beneath the armpits and her arms glowed a raw red. Chucking his fag butt onto the gravel, he went over to her: 'Tell Yoshi I've gone for a piss, if he asks anything,' he murmured, taking care not to be overheard. They'd had a lecture from the guide about never straying from the party, but the coach loos seemed built for twelve year olds and the blue plastic affair near the camel gave off a foul whiff.

She said nothing and did not look up. The fan flackered momentarily against the brim of her hat.

He lumbered away, gearing himself up for the reprimand from the tour guide that he expected at any minute: 'Oh, Mr Fergusson!' And the sad smile: you Europeans are so innocent. Yoshi and all the rest of them were full of blether about jihadists and stranger-danger. Edward winced with a mixture of anger and embarrassment, but then felt oddly bereft when there was no call. He was afraid and, because he was afraid, he had to look around whatever corners might present themselves. The unknown was always the greatest fear. He rehearsed yet again in his head the lines for the flight home: I told you we shouldn't have gone. That girl. She wasn't guarding. Guards looked around. Walked around. Checked.

A heavy man of fifty nine in Panama hat, white jacket and fawn trousers, he was conscious of crumpled clothes, shirt hanging out at the back and a dull ache in his gut. The only times now when his body felt truly comfortable was when he was lying in bed. He climbed a slope and found himself on top of a shallow ravine with, beyond it, the vast and stony desert, eternal beneath a china-blue sky in which lodged the yellow sun. His spirit lightened at the unexpected view and he counted to twenty before easing himself crab-like down the scree and into the bed of the dried-up wadi. At the bottom, he dusted his hands on his trousers and then wiped his trousers with a handkerchief. The place was about a dozen feet wide and the banks were the same height. Standing with feet absurdly wide apart, he pissed. The splashing of the water deepened the surrounding silence. The coach party might have been a thousand miles away. He was tired, acid burned in his gut and his heart thumped. 'Lose five stone and stop smoking or you won't make seventy,' Doctor MacTavish had said. Odious little man. What gave doctors the right to tell people how to live? And that Saint Andrews flag on the wall. What was that all about? He was getting worked up and those black shadows were appearing at the corners of his eyes. He knew he should sit down, but ironically the anger made him resist. The path of the ravine meandered around a corner. Edward glanced at his watch and took a Rennie. He walked and listened to the stones crackling against the edge of silence. 'I am a man,' he said. 'Free. So I'm walking. That's what you do. If you face your fears head on, they dissolve like mist in sunshine. You walk.'

After a short time, his Facebook Post philosophy started to shrivel. He was bored and unwell. Better not die right now. Imagine dying when you were bored! Dying would just intensify that waste of time. Heat, dust, stones, blue sky. No view. No jihadis. 'Postcard to Tim and Miranda and e mail B.A. about that coffee,' he said. 'Your coffee was like old socks,' – yes, that would be good: slightly humorous but also forceful. He'd make the point too about not wanting compensation – none of this affecting-hurt bollocks that everyone went in for these days. 'And a card to Simon Barton – good diplomacy. Well done, that thought.' Why do I say some thoughts but only think others? 'I should have spent another twenty minutes on that Windward-Sams order. Got it finished. ' Would Mrs Benson really come in twice a day to pull the curtains and turn the lights on and off?

Edward tutted, cross at the thinking that took him away from a moment that he should at least try to enjoy. A fragment of the score to Lawrence of Arabia drifted in his mind. Or was it Born Free? How did you tell? Sweat itched out of his skin.

A giant boulder offered a segment of shade. Edward approached it and crouched in the shadow. Stay here five minutes, then get on back. He checked his watch again. Hunkered low and breathed. The silence was like being in the presence of an enormous, invisible beast.

Presently, however, he became aware of delicate sounds: the shifting of his clothes when he moved to ease a ruck in his boxer shorts, the creaking of body fluids; and also something else. He bent his head. Listened. No? No, there was something. Tiny black nudges of sound. What were they? The wind through stone hollows? There was no wind. Perhaps the freak transportation of chatter from the coach party? The shifty movements of terrorists? He'd joke about all this later. Make up some sort of story. Holding a glass of white wine in the back garden, the barbecue going. It sounded like water. Some of these wadis experienced flash floods following winter rains in distant mountains: he'd seen a film on YouTube: a trickle of water flowing down a dry river bed then suddenly a vast flood.

He stood up quickly, looking for an easy spot to climb. And was startled to see a black, long-eared goat. The animal stopped and regarded him with lugubrious eyes before trotting on. Edward looked round. A scattered herd of the bleating creatures was coming towards him in a cloud of sun-filled dust and, behind them, a figure in a black robe.

The goats swarmed around and he was surrounded by blaring and wailing, thick dust and the stench of rotting carpet. Edward held a handkerchief to his face, but took it away again to offer a smile at the approaching figure. He was conscious that this was a generous gesture: another person might have been annoyed by these bloody animals and show fear at the approach of an Arab. Not him. He was English. And, after all, they had every right to be here. The goatherd was a boy of about seventeen. He held a long staff and around his shoulders was slung a hairy water bladder.

'Good afternoon!' said Edward, conscious of holding his ground and acting the polite Englishman in the desert. The boy would appreciate his being treated like a normal person and not a crazed jihadist. Edward pointed to the bladder and said something about it looking like a giant's bollock. The office joker.

The boy, face expressionless, held it out. It was stopped with a clay plug. Edward approached. The boy's hands were strong and dusty, fingernails bitten. They'd never held a pen. Edward felt a waft of warm air from the space between the boy's jellaba and his skin: musky and oddly stirring. It was a scent that seemed to suggest a real life that he had never had, a life not stopped by soaps and scrubs and showers. The image of an ancient, candlelit carpeted cave flashed through his mind and was gone. He raised the bladder to his lips. The water was warm and rancid so he spat it out but nevertheless continued to pour the grateful wetness over his face. It smelt uriney, but cool splashes beneath his shirt felt wonderful. He took off his hat and jacket and splashed the water on his head, half-appalled to find that he could not stop. He poured until the bladder was empty.

The boy was sitting on a low rock. Edward held his arms away from his body to help the drying. 'I'm amazed,' he said. 'I wouldn't have thought there's anything for goats to graze on, here.'

The boy spat a few gristly words in Arabic. He had a face that might be drawn using just a few thin lines. His eyes were a piercing blue and light tangled in his jet black curls. There was a shadowy moustache on his upper lip.

'There must be underground water nearby,' said Edward, putting his hat and jacket back on. 'Or an oasis. Do you come from a village? It never rains here, does it? Mm? No, you don't understand, do you? No comprendos? If I was here by myself I'd hire you on the spot. You could be my guide. Show me the secret Negev that us Westerners never see on our package hols. Speak you English? Comprendos Inglese? No.'

The boy produced an apple and bit into the crispy green skin with white teeth. He ignored the man and watched the goats tugging and nibbling at low clumps of dry grass.

'I wish I was that apple,' Edward said. 'Or an orange,' he followed quickly. 'Cool's what I mean.' He took off his hat. Passed his fingers through his hair. Fanned himself. The drying water was turning his shirt to cardboard. 'You've got a nice life here.'

The boy plainly did not understand a word. Maybe he was an idiot. Edward looked hard at him, but turned away quickly when the boy flicked his eyes in his direction and stared frankly.

'You've got eyes like a young animal. You really don't speak English? Mm? En-gliss? What – your – name – is? Me – Edwarrrd. No understanding. You look cool. Well done. Do you swim? What's the time? God, quarter past already. Shit. I must cut along, because we're not getting very far in this conversation. If we'd had time, I'd've asked you to take me to the oasis where you swim. You could pose for me.' Instinctively his hand felt for the phone in his pocket. 'You'd do that, wouldn't you? Against the rocks. This is the Arab boy I met a hundred miles down from Be'er Sheva. He didn't speak, but we connected... No, I don't think I was especially brave. You have to talk to the people when you go to these places. Most of them are quite normal, actually.'

And then it happened. Quite suddenly, like a squall on a hitherto calm day at sea.

'Please don't stare at me like that.' Edward kept a quiet, matter-of-fact tone and an inconsequential smile, although now he felt his scalp tingle with rage. How dare he? They were all the same. 'All the boys try that on here. You effing people. You stick to your goats. Slaughter them yourself do you? Get them between your legs, and slit the throat so the blood spurts. I know what it's like. I'll bet you yell, too, while you're doing it. Eh? Practise for your effing beheadings. You love it, oh you love it, making you hard like a man. You're all sexually frustrated is why you turn to terror. All this gun stuff is just metaphor don't think we don't know. Stroking the rifle butt and shooting and making that orgasmic war cry you've got. Your smug faces grinning at the camera.'

Edward talked calmly, the goats grazed and the boy's tongue and teeth prepared the apple for his stomach.

The boy threw aside the apple core.

Edward regarded it. His skin tightened and heart raced.

The boy stood up. Suddenly there was a mobile phone in his hand. Fuck! Who was he going to call? Edward's insides filled with cold terror. How had he been so confident that the kid didn't understand English? Idiot. He saw a picture of himself on the News in an orange jumpsuit. He tried to run but was frozen. He drew out his own phone and held it poised theatrically ready to tap the emergency number. IDF helicopters could be here in minutes. Don't try it matey.

But the boy just glanced at the phone, put it back in his pocket, shouted at the goats and moved on. Boy and goats swirled past the man like an indifferent river and Edward just wasn't prepared for the extraordinary intense sorrow of it all. When they were some way ahead, 'Hey!' he called. 'Hey!' It was a cry of passion.

The boy stopped and looked back without interest, his face in clear focus amongst the blur of dust and light. Out with his goats one day he had passed a foreigner.

'You?' Edward asked as the boy turned away again.

Edward picked up a stone. It was filled with power: not old, dead rock but alive with potential.

The boy walked on.

The stone hit the boy in the back. Or, perhaps, just missed; not, after all, being possessed of any authority. It was merely something that had moved clumsily and too heavily from one place to another. Like a life in that aspect, at least. The boy didn't even notice.

The man was concentrated fury. He picked up something else that had fallen; then, with a yell, ran forward. He passed the boy, and some goats spread before him along the rocky track. 'Yalla! Yalla! Yalla!' the man's shouts mingled amongst airy bleats. The goats fled in all directions. 'There – now try to fucking find them.'

And there he was again in the car park. How had that happened? He flapped his arms at the goats, as if trying to round them up. The boy had disappeared.

The tourists, tidied up into the coach again and locked behind dark windows, watched thin, black goats pursued by a fat, white man. They all had stories about each other. Edward halted and the goats settled into another arrangement. He saw Maria watching him. Her gaze was tired. My husband chasing goats. It wasn't important.

'Trying to help catch them,' he explained, panting as he stepped past the soldier girl and into the coach. 'Hopeless.' The aisle was cold.

Yoshi said, 'Mr Fergusson, I... .'

'Yes-yes-yes... .' He headed quickly to his seat.

They had all been waiting for him. He made a jokey face: puckering his cheeks and raising his eyebrows.

The driver started up immediately, causing the bus to shudder and a woman yelped. 'Not a fucking bomb, dear,' Edward muttered, slightly too loudly.

The bus moved on and Edward saw the boy again, steadily gathering his herd together: a desert scene gradually receding through the window, and then pulled abruptly away as they turned a bend. Gone forever.

An appalling sense of loss made Edward think that he had not yet screamed enough, and he bit his lower lip. But the feeling passed. If necessary, he could always take an extra Prozac that night. The thought gave him deep comfort. Presently, he and Maria would doze off, and he would wake her so that she might give him a couple of Anadin from her handbag. ('I told you to get Anadin Extra, you know these ordinary ones don't work for me.') But pain confirmed his existence. He welcomed it. Sometimes, he sensed the deeper rhythm beneath the awkward jerkiness of his heart: alive, in pain; alive, in pain; alive, in pain. It all helped, and took the pressure off other areas. Some day, with arthritis and artificial hip, he would sit on the front at Brighton and know that there was nothing else he could be doing. The promise of physical decay offered a certain relief. There was, after all, always the future where you could just sit and eat and drink at intervals before sleep. The tv might show you a rainforest. Or a bear in the Rockies.

Maria offered him a Rennie. It was a token of peace. They got along all right.

'If I so much as see another falafel,' she said.

'And sheep's milk cheese,' he added.

'Their tomatoes are really acid.'

'I might give that Gaviscon a go when we get back.'

'Rene swears by it.'

'Has to be worth a try.'

'Liquid or tablets?'

'Tablets.'

He saw them on the supermarket shelf.

'Rene gagged on the liquid.'

'I remember her saying.'

In his trouser pocket, he felt the apple core oozing damp against his skin like the lick of a warm tongue and he knew that he would never throw it away. He would hide it somewhere even when it was dry and shrivelled and he would take it out now and again and examine the bite marks and maybe even put it in his mouth and try to make it moist. Picturing the future moments he experienced a strange and awful joy.

Rachael Smart

Rachael Smart has a thing about words. Recent work has been published at Ink, Sweat and Tears, Prole, and Coast to Coast to Coast. She has an MA in Creative Writing from The University of Nottingham [With Distinction] and is thigh-deep in a hybrid collection about discontinued lipsticks. Rachael writes for The Motherload and helps coordinate their book club. She also reviews books for STORGY. She rides a retro bike [with a basket.]

The Inconsequential Codes on Lipsticks

900. red alert

The first time you are sat in geography trying to grasp the distinctions between finite and infinite. You have the same trouble with fiction and non-. When a word is the same as its synonym, give or take a few letters, it muddies your head but you reckon you've cracked the labels on the cross-section of sedimentary rock.

Something solid brushes up against your shoulders. It feels like a hand. It is a hand: a beefy and hot one that trespasses round the back of you, making contact with the cool cotton of your blouse and the skin concealed beneath. Before you can spin round your bra strap is twanged so hard that the elastic snaps against the middle of your back and the waspish sting takes your breath. One of the boys on the table behind does a deliberately subdued clap of approval so that only you can hear it. You don't turn round to witness the rise of macho canned laughter. Instead, you raise your hand, considering the least humiliating words you can tell it with, and Crouch looks up from his desk with bullish eyes that look vast behind retro glasses.

What is it?

Sir, one of the boys on the table behind just touched me.

Touched you? Do you want to expand? Whilst you pause to find the words he sharpens a yellow pencil briskly with abrupt twists and after pulling it out, closely inspects the hole and blows hard on the pencil's graphite tip.

Pulled at my strap. You know, Sir. Through my shirt.

I see. And are you surprised?

Surprised?

I mean, is it really that surprising going by the muck on your face?

Muck, sir? Your mind feels white and jellied by the shock of what is emerging.

I mean that red stuff on your lips.

Your brain has difficulty correlating a link between the invasion of privacy and that morning's hurried smear of lip gloss.

Do you know what lipstick's meant to emulate?

You don't answer. Feel conscious of your cheeks flushing up, your heart doing a runaway in the cage of your chest.

Cleopatra wore red on her lips to simulate the engorged vulva during intercourse. Red was also a firm favourite of Ladies of the Night. If you're not sure of that euphemism, I suggest you look it up. Lipstick is a clear invitation.

The table behind ruptures with a rush of laughter as the boys sense that they are off the hook. All the girls in the class become ultra-interested in their sandstone specimens and their clasped hands and the pale blue line graph pattern on the desk.

Sir, I thought this was geography not biology, and even as you say it, your voice sounds reedy and dislocated, and you know that it is neither. This subject that has no name.

This subject of boys touching you. Crouch facilitating it, and the girls, the mutest of girls not one of whom has got your back. You realise that this new curriculum you are encountering is something else entirely. Non-fiction and boundless. The fault line that's in every structure. It threatens to break you.

500. revolution red

In A-Level Communication Studies you undertake a group analysis of a billboard poster. The gaunt model wears a white bikini to drink a glass of milk indoors. She sits cross-legged on kitchen tiles with a pair of red thermal socks pulled right the way up to her walnut-brown knees and has to raise her chin to meet the camera's eye. There are white milky stalagmites encrusted on her top lip. Tributaries of blueish semi-skimmed have run from the corners of her mouth down her neck and pooled glacial white in the craters of her décolletage. Her nipples are erect under triangles of Lycra. The glass is static in her hands but milk bombs out from the top of the glass in a shower of creamy meteors.

When your teacher asks your table for feedback, you tell him that you think the advert smacks of some bloke's sexual fantasy. He widens his eyes and pushes you for more: you point out her subordinate floor position and the illogical fact of her being undressed merely to have a drink. You say that the milk explosion might be how a man perceives his climax [an exaggerated one, you laugh] and isn't that semen residue around her mouth? Surely, you say, the catchphrase Got a lotta bottle must be a pun on a man's virility? He rolls his eyes and raises one side of his top lip to appeal quizzically to some of your peers.

What do we think, lads?

There is silence.

No takers on that argument, I'm afraid, he says. Personally, I think you're reading way too much in to it.

At lunch, he catches up with you in the car park and tells you that your intellect really excites him. He says he felt you were really trying to connect with him in today's class but there's a time and a place for that kind of stuff and can you foresee any issues in resuming the conversation over coffee?

051. muse red

During an apprenticeship at a local newspaper, you have a fling with your mentor who has all the hallmarks of being a keeper. An older man. Educated. A published crime writer with a background in sports journalism. He says good things about your writing and doesn't speak to your breasts. Plus, you like his tousled hair and its uncooperative direction of growth and the grainy tendons in his forearms when he types. He talks intellectual sense about the gender disparities in publishing and supports anonymous applications to get more women into senior management roles.

It is too bad when you find out that he likes it rough. He confesses to liking some pretty weird shit early on and because you are both trying to identify what makes the other hot and turn to fluid, you're game to please. The sex feels like a sickness. It isn't that he hurts you. But it's acting out all the bits leading up to hurt. That vacuum of silence in his master bedroom when you don't know what's coming. Being tied up. Unable to see where he is when he's not touching you. Having to pretend not to consent to what he does. He asks you to say no like you mean it and even though it's a self-betrayal to blur those lines you acquiesce.

There are other things – beautiful things: he makes you soft buttery eggs in the mornings and strokes your eyebrows until you fall asleep. He applies arnica cream gently to the little marks he leaves behind: a Parma violet anklet, an embroidery of pressed lilacs around your wrists.

There are films, too. Ones he insists you watch with him at first. Films starring girls much younger than you. They all have similarly soft, bell-shaped breasts and look surprised when they get squirted on. You tell him the films are really not your thing, and he's OK with that, says he only really watches to get warmed up.

One evening you are both half-cut over a bottle of wine and some vodka shots, and you say too much in the last pub. Tell him that the porn troubles you. That there's something inherently wrong about a man of a certain age needing to watch girls of a certain age and you tell him you can't help but see the human beyond the pixelated images, that it's the same way you view a butcher's window: hyper aware of how a pig goes from living to not.

He says he is offended. He makes apostrophe marks with his forefingers each time he says the word offended to reinforce the severity of your slur. Can't you see, he hisses, that he's worlds apart from the sort of perverts who have underage sex? Those sorts of men repulse him. Especially the ones with daughters. He'd never lay a finger on a girl, he needs you to understand that.

A week on, he says he's gutted but he'll have to call time on the apprenticeship. The company is restructuring and making redundancies. It wouldn't do to keep you on. In the team meeting he talks about how talented you are and refers to the quality of your content. Before you clear your desk, he gives you a signed copy of his new (hardback) thriller, says what a pleasure it's been showing you the ropes.

053. retro red

Shortly after you qualify as a social worker you get a high-profile case involving child grooming. In a meeting with police and school you share that two thirteen-year-old girls have been seen wearing new clothes: expensive designer dresses they could never afford to buy themselves. Luxury lipsticks, too. Christian Dior, Chanel. Brands you only usually see in high-end magazines. One of the two male DI's sitting next to you turns to his colleague; the porkiest one with a purpling nose. He shields his mouth with one toady hand and says perfectly audibly: that pair always dress like they're asking for it.

In the thick silence that follows you will think about those girls and many times after; girls from the estate who hitch up their navy skirts and nick lipstick testers from the precinct. Girls who have not started their periods yet. Girls who would feel sassy as Lady Ga Ga in their new gear with their satin-look lips. You look down at the water stains on your boots, a portrait of rain dried in to the suede and you are unable to articulate all the wrong in that room, and operating outside on the slick streets of Concrete City.

When you report the DI's comment to your manager he shakes his head as though you are misguided at best, at worst petty. He says surely you wouldn't want to squeal about an off-the-cuff comment like that and aren't the police thin enough on the ground as it is?

The girls go missing a week later. Months after, one of the mothers tells you that the cruellest thing for her is when the landline rings. That micro window of hope that comes on a surge of white adrenalin, that it might be one of them wanting a lift from some phone box out in the sticks and during windy nights when the loose glass in the shed windows rattle, that's got to be the cruellest, she says, because she imagines it's the click of her daughter's key in the back door lock.

On the wintery morning that the findings of the Rotherham Inquiry are broadcast on the BBC news, the reporter uses the words 'police' and 'complicit in abuse' in the same sentence and when your percolated coffee comes back up into the kitchen sink – still warm – it's the colour of clay mud and builder's dust, and something else you can't name.

Susan Utting

Susan Utting began writing short stories and poems while studying for an English degree. She subsequently worked for 17 years as creative writing tutor at Reading University, eventually specialising in poetry writing. Her poems have been widely published and anthologised and she has four full poetry collections. *Half the Human Race: New & Selected Poems* is her latest, published by Two Rivers Press. She currently lives and works as a freelance tutor and poet in Berkshire. www. susanutting.com

Good as Gold

You worry about them right from the start really. Well, before that, soon as you're sure you've really fallen, soon as Doctor Brown tells you what you already know. Even then you think, will they be, you know, *all right* – normal, all there. And the first thing you do when you get them is you check – count the fingers and toes; look at their backs. But then you can check everything on the outside, but you can't really know what's going on inside, can you? You don't think of that. You can't be expected to know anyway, like Connie says, it's not as if we're trained or anything, and even the doctors couldn't have known, not then. And when they did, they couldn't do anything. Poor little mite. But you'd think a mother'd know, wouldn't you? I should've spotted it. And sometimes, I think, when I look back, I *did* know all along, really. There was something different. The signs were there, but I just didn't want to see it.

Like that time one Sunday up the allotment. Lovely day it was, not a cloud in the sky, sun blazing down fit to scorch you. I remember it because she had her sun hat on – that one with the yellow lazy-daisies I'd just finished off, with the satin stitch edging. I'd just finished it that morning and she'd sat so still and good getting ready to go out, there on the draining board while I'd given her a lick and a promise and tied the ribbons up under her chin in a big white bow. Well anyway, this day Ted tells her to get off his seed bed. Quite

sharp with her he was. Mind you, he always was a stickler for behaviour. She
was only pushing the earth about with the toe of her sandal, bless her, how
was she to know he'd just raked it ready for his brassica seedlings? Suppose
she just thought it was like a sandpit, for playing in, couldn't resist the flatness
of it, just waiting to be jumped in, scooped and patted into pies and patterns.
She used to love helping me with the baking like that – give her a bit of left
over pastry to play with, a dusting of flour and she'd be happy as anything for
hours. So he has a right go at her – *Get off there, you bad girl! You get back on
that path and stay there and don't you move till I tell you to!*

That's the thing really. She never was a bad girl. Good as gold. Always.
Unnatural, Connie says, and I suppose she's right in a way. Not that she said
anything at the time. Anyway, this time I was clearing up the cups and bits
and sorting out the picnic bag and I'd gone round the back of the allotment
sheds to rinse the cups out under the tap and old Lofty was there and we got
to chatting about this and that. His wife hadn't been too well again, terrible
with her nerves and migraines – absolutely exhausts her, well both of them
really, him having to do everything in the house as well as all the rest. Well,
I must've been quite a while – he does go on a bit, Lofty, and you've got to
sympathize, haven't you? So when I got back there she is, stood quite still,
just where she'd been before, where Ted told her to. Course, he's forgotten
all about it, too busy with his seeds and that to even notice. Didn't look as
if she'd moved a muscle in all that time and in all that heat. Quite red she
was, her little arms all scorched and blotchy, her face like it always was – a bit
serious, deep looking. Not unhappy, just serious. Kind of funny under that
pretty bonnet. You never did know what she was thinking. But she hadn't
moved in all that time. Done just as she'd been told. Good as gold. You
might say too good, really.

I should've seen it then. Poor little mite. And there's us so proud of how
well behaved she was – you could take her anywhere, anywhere at all and

she'd be no trouble to anyone – perfect, that's it, real perfect. Just shows, you can't tell, can you, even a mother can't be knowing that, illnesses and stuff. Like Connie says, I've nothing to blame myself for. Nothing at all, really. Though I sometimes think – well you can't help thinking, can you – I think I really should've known something wasn't quite right. She did look nice in that bonnet, though, bless her cotton socks. Kind of quaint in an old-fashioned sort of way.

It was all right on the day, Nice weather, nothing sad about it. Blue skies and sunshine all the way! I'd wanted Eric there. He had the right sort of face – jolly, a bit red, chubby cheeks and that, couldn't look tragic if he tried. Him, Phil and Lofty and the others, strapping fellows, all of them, to carry her. Got my way on that one, anyway! Ted had dug his heels in about the flowers and he was right, really – they don't last. Give the money to the hospital, their need's greater, show our gratitude and that, that's what he said. Then afterwards, when we got back to the house, I don't know what I'd expected. Ted was always a quiet one – a doer not a talker, you know the sort, just got on with it, that was his way. But I wish he'd asked me. Or told me. Less of a shock then. I'd expected everything to be the same, just like it was when we'd left the house. But everything had gone – her toys, clothes and stuff, that musical box with a pop-up ballerina that played Brahms Lullaby. Got her to sleep nicely that did. And all the photos. All gone, even her little bed, the lot. He'd had someone in and cleared it all out. He meant it for the best, I know that. Thought it would help if there wasn't anything to remind me. As if I could wipe it all out. Forget, just like that.

No, not one for conversation, Ted. Not like me and Connie – hind legs off donkeys when we're together. Don't know what I'd have done without Connie. She understood, walked me to the shops and that when I couldn't go on the bus. Just too much to take, buses. The sides closed in on me, it went dark in my head and I'd have get off. Jumped off when it was moving once, grazed my knees real bad. She didn't fuss, just understood. *Let's just walk*, she'd say, *nice day for it, never mind buses, it'll do us good.* And she'd pop round to see if I was all right – never said so much – *just passing*, she'd say, then get stuff out the pantry for me, or the cupboard under the stairs when I couldn't go in there.

Took a while but I'm all right now. Go in quite small spaces on my own, to fetch stuff. So long as I leave the door open, can see the way out. So long as there's plenty of light. And we talk about it a bit, about her, every now and again, Connie and me. Just natural like, like you'd talk about anyone who's gone. Not sad, really. Just funny little things she used to do and say. Quite grown up with her words, she was. Told me to be careful dusting round my china bits and bobs once, *fragile*, she said! Her only three years old, knowing a word like that! But then she always was quick, picked things up easy. Good job I've got Connie. And I've got a photo now – she gave me the one off her mantelpiece. The snap of her sitting on the pouffe. She's wearing her gingham frock. She loved that frock, the puffed sleeves trimmed with white piping. A devil to get those sleeves set in right, mind you. Took me for ever. Stood my ground on that one, on the photo, I did. Gave Ted one of my looks, bold as brass, just stood it up, right in the middle of the sideboard. Pride of place! Didn't say a word.

Her room's been done out like a guest room now, fresh paint, all new furniture, curtains. Same bit of carpet, though – *good as new*, I told him, *no need replacing it.* Thing is, there's four dips in it, in the pile, where her little bed stood. Still there they are, the marks, underneath the new bed. So they don't show. I know they're there though. Go up and have a peep some days when I'm in on my own. Just lift up the edges of the bedspread and look at them. Get right under there some days. You'd think I'd have one of my turns, dark little place like that, under a bed. But I don't. Not a bit of it. Gives me a sort of warm, nice feeling under there. Safe, if you know what I mean. Seeing them still there somehow, touching them, stroking those flat smooth little dips in the pile. Curl up tight and run my fingers over them, over and over, gentle like. Funny how it takes you, really. Like Connie says, takes all sorts.

Julianne Woodside

Julianne Woodside is a writer living in Sacramento, CA. Her poetry has appeared in the Tule Review. Her fiction has appeared in *The Farallon Review*, was performed at Stories on Stage Sacramento, and placed second in the Writer's and Editor's Network 2018 Short Story competition. Her creative non-fiction has been featured in numerous letters and emails. When not writing, she enjoys rescuing stray cats, cooking and volunteering at local theatres. She is currently working on short stories and a memoir collection.

If, Say

If, say, you were perched on a tree branch outside your house, with your half-naked legs freezing under your skirt because you forgot to put on your brother's hand-me-down wool snow pants, with your socks all wet and your hands so numbing cold you're sort of worried about how you'll eventually climb down, and

if, say, you were just a few weeks shy of your ninth birthday and had climbed the gnarled old tree an hour ago, even though your mother says girls shouldn't climb trees and even though it's winter and the leaves are gone so it doesn't hide you out on that one perfect branch where you're waiting, the one that lets you see into your kitchen with its old icebox and the shiny new Silex on the stove, and

if, maybe, you were up there on a Sunday night when your father gets home late, so late, from what he always says is "mechanic school," where he goes every other weekend and which you didn't suspect was anything else, although you did wonder why your mother cried in their room with the door closed after he left, even though he went there to learn how to do a better job at the garage where he fixes people's broken cars and earns the money to put food on the table and give his children a decent education, and

if, say, you were up there freezing and wanting with all your heart for your father to come home, to come home this night the way he's always come home, to hug you and to laugh with you, to tickle you and be your hero who isn't afraid of anything and who knows everything there is to know about cars and stars and homework and how to tie fancy knots and who taught you to swim and to climb that tree, and who loves you and your mother and your brothers and sister, and maybe you just desperately wanted everything to be the same but it wasn't because, well, maybe because

this is the first time you've waited for your dad to come back home after your older sister told you that your father's "mechanic school" was really him staying with another woman in the town across the river.

And what if this was also

after you hit your sister in the stomach really hard for telling you such a giant fib, and she pushed you away and laughed at you for being a Dumb Dora and believing in the big old rotten liar that is your father, because your sister heard it from her best friend Diane because Diane had to go spend the weekend with her aunt in that town across the river, and Diane knows your dad because she sees him in front of your house washing the car and mowing the lawn, but there across the river was your dad in front of her aunt's neighbor's house, the one her aunt calls a floozy, and he was mowing the lawn there, and then sat outside on the stoop with his arm around that floozy, and that was when he was supposed to be in mechanic school.

And

if, say, your sister had suddenly stopped yelling, and looked really sad, and said she was sorry, really sorry she told you, because she's known since summer and you're too little and it would kill Mother that you know because you're the baby, and don't tell anybody what she told you,

well,

that's probably why you forgot the snow pants when you ran outside and climbed your tree.

So, let's just say you are curled up there in the almost dark, with your frozen fingers and your ears hurting so fierce you can't tell if they've stopped working because of the cold, or maybe it's just that the kitchen window is closed and the snow has clobbered down the sound so all you can hear is your heartbeat and your stupid sniffling, because maybe you can't stop crying watching your hero father who finally came home, who bizarrely looks exactly the same even though he isn't a hero anymore, and you watch him come into the lit-up kitchen where your mother sits at the table in her pink housedress and the soft blue sweater that you love. She has a cup of coffee you watched her pour from her wonderful new coffee-maker half an hour ago, but that she hasn't taken even one sip from, and you keep watching as your father drops his coat and takes off his boots and comes over to her, where he leans over the table and gently takes her hands and starts kissing them one at a time. He's looking up at her face with that expression you remember from when he wanted you to dive into the deep end of the pool where he was waiting with his arms up in the air, and now he slowly walks around the table, his mouth still talking, his dark hair falling into his eyes as he works his lips up to her wrists and you watch her turn her face into his like they are going to kiss and

maybe that's when you let go of your pee because you can't hold it anymore, so you close your eyes and stuff your thumb in your mouth to stop your crying while the pee is all warm and then it gets cold, so cold and then,

then they aren't in the kitchen anymore.

After that, maybe a long times passes, and it's after your bedtime, and you hear them calling and calling for you, but you still don't leave your tree.

And maybe, when finally your older brother thinks to come outside looking for you, you tell him to go away but when your rotten liar father comes out you're glad he still loves you and wants to rescue you out of the tree that you're too frozen to climb down from, and even though you want to yell at him to go away he climbs up to help you, and you're so mad at him you're just a little bit happy that he has to touch your cold pee when he carries you in, and everyone crowds into the bathroom, so worried about you and your shaking blue fingers and lips,

and then maybe your sister is so worried she's crying, and then she starts yelling at your dad that if you die of the cold it'll be all his fault, because she told you about his fake mechanic school, and your father's face looks like he swallowed soap, he goes all pale and lost looking. He keeps saying "I thought you wouldn't know! You're not supposed to know!" and then he cries and your mother cries and your brothers are yelling "What does she know?!" and your father starts yelling to leave you alone and that scares you and makes you happy at the same time and you try to keep your thumb in your mouth right through your mother peeling your clothes off and putting you in the tub and you don't complain like you normally would about the hot cold pains in your legs and your ears as they warm up.

And maybe your dad says to your mother, right there in the bathroom in front of you, that he will quit going to mechanic school, except he has to go one more time to tell her because she deserves that much, and his face looks like he's almost as miserable as you are, and your mother says "Finally" and cries some more, and she bends down and hugs you really hard and you think, maybe you knowing about your dad isn't going to kill her after all, but after they leave the bathroom you stay in the water for a very long time until your brothers start pounding on the door.

After you get out of the tub, you go right to bed without asking to stay up or getting a snack because nothing is normal tonight and anyway you don't want to see your father when he comes back from a walk he said he was taking, and your mother comes to tuck you in and hugs you extra hard and whispers "thank you," and you're not sure exactly why but it's nice anyway, and you don't think you can sleep but you do.

In the morning you give your sister your favorite magic stone and you won't tell her why but it's because she didn't want you to die from the cold, and your mother sings while she makes pancakes for breakfast even though it's Monday, and when you say your feet still feel funny from freezing, she lets you stay home from school and the two of you sit together on the couch and read A Little Princess and play Old Maid, even though it's a kid's game and your mother is a little bored but she stays with you all day and she even makes you laugh a little.

But what if, when your father comes home in his dirty grey mechanic shirt just in time for dinner, you see your mother smile at him like it's any other day, and your sister gives you a big thumbs up behind his back when he's hugging her and then he reaches out to give you a hug, too, then,

maybe you suddenly feel a really big pain in your chest and you feel like maybe it's a little hard to breathe because you remember how you were glad to see him every other day of your life but now he's not a hero and what you want to do is hit him in the stomach really hard but he's holding out his arm for a hug from you, and you wonder if he went to see the floozy one more time today? or will it be tomorrow? and what about being a rotten liar and what about eating dinner looking at him and why isn't anyone else still mad at him and

you jump off the couch and go get your brother's hand-me-down snow pants

and go outside to climb your tree

but this time you climb out the other way, out on the other branch over the fence where you look over the neighbor's yard, and you think maybe you could build a shelf up there to stash some sandwiches and maybe a book, and a pair of mittens if, say, you forget them again tomorrow. Because, it's possible, you just might have to stay up there for a very long time.

Judges' Profiles

Kate Johnson (Chair)

Kate is a literary agent at the New York-based Mackenzie Wolf literary agency, representing a range of fiction and non-fiction writers across the US and the UK, including short story writers Sam Allingham, Tania Hershman, Bryan Hurt, Bonnie Nadzam, Hasanthika Sirisena and Azareen Van der Vliet Oloomi.

Lucy Cowie

Lucy is a freelance editor with over a decade's experience working with a broad range of fiction and non-fiction writers. She started her publishing career at the literary agency LAW and Penguin Random House, before heading to the West Country where she continues to edit for publishers as well as independent writers.

Roshi Fernando

Roshi is the winner of the 2009 Impress Prize and the author of the acclaimed short story collection, *Homesick* (Bloomsbury). She has a PhD in Creative Writing and lectures on short stories. She was shortlisted for the 2011 *Sunday Times* EFG Short Story Award and longlisted for the Frank O'Connor International Short Story Prize in the same year.

Polly Ho-Yen

Polly is the author of three novels for children, which have been nominated for numerous awards including the Carnegie Medal, Waterstones Children's Book Prize and the Blue Peter Book Award. She worked in publishing for several years and has also been a teacher. As well as a writer, she is currently Reader Development Librarian for Bristol Libraries.

Acknowledgements

We are extremely indebted to the fantastic people below whose time, expertise and overwhelming kindness have ensured that this year's competition has been a joyous experience and have enabled us to publish a brilliant anthology:

The judging panel – Kate Johnson (chair), Lucy Cowie, Roshi Fernando, and Polly Ho-Yen. Our readers – Diane Becker, Jo Darque, Katherine Hanks, Lu Hersey, Richard Jones, Mike Manson, Bertel Martin, Eleanor Pender, Dawn Pomroy, Tom Robinson, Pam Smallwood. Chris Hill, Jonathan Ward, Valentina Vinci and the 3rd year Illustration students at University of the West of England. Tangent Books; Bristol Libraries; Foyles; Peter Morgan and Mark Furneval at ScreenBeetle; Bristol 24/7; And Joe Burt, Sylvie Kruiniger, Rosa Lovegood, Eva Mason, Louis Melia, Natasha Melia, Dave Oakley, and Thomas Rasche.

Finally, and most importantly, a massive thank you to all the writers who submitted stories for the *2018 Bristol Short Story Prize*. Your work provided us with many hundreds of hours of eye-opening, inspiring and transformative reading.

2018
Bristol Short Story Prize
Longlist

(a-z by writer's name)

Annie Lowe – Jay Barnett

Chicken Heart – Aniqah Choudhri

Plastic People – Zoë Comyns

Havoc Shore – Maureen Cullen

English – Eleanor Duffy

Shapeshifting – L.O. Evans

Dogging – Jess Farr-Cox

Eddie Rekks – Adi Gal

The Making of Nancy – Stacey Gowland

What Remains – Pamela Hensley

Two Heads – Gary Hunter

Waste – Bethan James

The Cat Lady that Therefore I Am – Melanie Jones

Chestnut Avenue – Sarah Burton Kennedy

Goodbye, Mr Penguin – Shibani Lal

The Significance of Swans – Rhiannon Lewis

Fresh Watter – Rob McInroy

A Beginner's Guide to Stammering – Rosemary Mairs

You are Here – Dana Miltins

Blue Slushy at the Red Rooster – Sarah Starr Murphy

Staff Announcement – Valerie O'Riordan

Ellen – Christopher Owen

Dinan – Noa Padawer-Blatt

There's a Place – Martin Pevsner

The Sack of Rice – Rizwan Piracha

The Road Home – Ian Priestley

Trespasser's Tide – David Rea

Transposition – Helen Rye

Water in the Desert – Peter Slater

The Inconsequential Codes on Lipsticks – Rachael Smart

Your Turn – Kailash Srinivasan

Little Yellow Planes – Zeus Sumra

Cowboy Boot – Dizz Tate

Good as Gold – Susan Utting

The Cardigan – Simon van der Velde

#Blesséd – Kate Ward

Powerful Owl – Chloe Wilson

The Sky Polisher – Katy Wimhurst

If, Say – Julianne Woodside

Strange Things – Safiya Ismaila Yero

Notable Contenders
These stories were in the running for the longlist until the final decisions were made

Great Barrier Reef – Sarah Barr

Land of Pine and Honey – Marie Gethins

Indigo – America Hart

Happy Birthday, Thomas Sankara! – Alexis Harvey

You Cannot Smell the Orange Trees – Rebecca F John

Cast Iron Grilles Painted Blue – Laura Lewis

Lifted – Sara Mang

Slippage – Johanna Robinson

The Horsemeat March – Matthew Rose

Robin's Fatal Flaw – Paul Sedgley

if found please return to – Tracey Slaughter

Carnival Day – Julie Twohig